Heartland™

A Winter's Gift

The seconds ticked by, and Amy's heart thumped painfully in her chest. She hoped she'd picked the right moment to give the mare a choice – the choice to defend her isolated freedom, or to put her trust in the human in the centre of the ring. Amy knew that for Flamenco, perhaps more than for any other horse she'd worked with, this was a major, life-changing decision that would lead her down a completely different path.

A murmur from the direction of the gate told Amy that the incredible was happening. Flamenco was walking towards her, and now she could hear the mare's soft footfalls on the sandy surface of the ring. A few seconds later, she felt Flamenco's breath on her neck and a velvety muzzle nudged her shoulder. Amy's heart gave a leap of joy.

Read all the books about Heartland:

Coming Home
After the Storm
Breaking Free
Taking Chances
Come What May
One Day You'll Know
Out of the Darkness
Thicker Than Water
Every New Day
Tomorrow's Promise
True Enough
Sooner or Later
Darkest Hour
Everything Changes
Love is a Gift
Holding Fast
A Season of Hope
Winter Memories (Special Edition)
New Beginnings
From This Day On
Always There
Amy's Journal (Special Edition)
Beyond the Horizon (Special Edition)

Heartland™

A Winter's Gift

Lauren Brooke

SCHOLASTIC

With special thanks to Gill Harvey

Scholastic Children's Books
An imprint of Scholastic Ltd
Euston House, 24 Eversholt Street
London, NW1 1DB, UK
Registered office: Westfield Road, Southam, Warwickshire, CV47 0RA
SCHOLASTIC and associated logos are trademarks and
or registered trademarks of Scholastic Inc.
Series created by Working Partners

First published in the US by Scholastic Inc, 2007
This edition published in the UK by Scholastic Ltd, 2008

ISBN 978 1407 10701 1

British Library Cataloguing-in-Publication Data
A CIP catalogue record for this book is available from the British Library

Printed in the UK by CPI Bookmarque, Croydon, CR0 4TD
Papers used by Scholastic Children's Books are made from wood grown in sustainable forests.

1 3 5 7 9 10 8 6 4 2

www.scholastic.co.uk/zone

Chapter One

Could this bus go any slower?

Amy Fleming peered out of the window, then at her watch, then out of the window again. It looked like they were moving at the same speed as the other vehicles; the bare winter trees whipped by along the motorway – forest, then farmland, then more forest and miles and miles of Virginia countryside. Amy sighed, leaned back on the headrest, and closed her eyes. It wasn't the bus that was crawling – it was time itself.

It seemed incredible that it was five months since she'd been at Heartland. She'd visited for a couple of weeks in early July, when she'd been all excited about her summer internship in Kentucky and had barely had time to get to know her new niece, Holly, before heading off again. She hadn't seen Ty then. He'd been on a road trip with friends, driving to Minnesota and back. Which meant that it was . . . Amy counted in her head . . . nine months since they'd seen each other. Nine months since they'd broken up. It felt like a lifetime.

And now it was already December 19 and there was less than a week until Christmas. Amy would be home for almost three weeks and she was so glad to be home in time to help get ready for the Heartland Christmas Eve open house. It was one of her favourite times of the year.

Amy's heart skipped a beat as she realized that the road had become familiar. They were finally entering her hometown. She gazed at the Christmas lights hanging across streets and then, as they neared the centre, watched shoppers struggle along the pavements laden down with bags of gifts. Only a few more moments now. . .

As the bus turned into the terminal, Amy leaped out of her seat to pull her backpack from the overhead rack. She was the first one off when the doors opened, bounding down the steps and looking around for the face she knew so well.

"Grandpa!" she cried, spying Jack Bartlett's white hair among the scattered group of families and friends who stood waiting.

Jack's face broke into a beaming smile. He hurried forward, enveloping her in a huge hug. "Amy, it's great to see you. We've missed you, honey."

Amy hugged him back, laughing. They stepped away from each other, and Jack grinned. "Looks like college life is suiting you," he said. "Though I daresay Nancy will want to fatten you up! Now, where's your suitcase?"

Amy rummaged among the pile of bags that the driver was lifting out of the storage compartment and found her battered case. She dragged it out of the way of the others, then paused to push her straight brown hair out of her eyes and hook it behind her ear. She had let it grow all summer so that it hung well below her shoulders, and she found herself wondering if Ty would like it. Then she reminded herself that they were friends and colleagues now, nothing more, and her hairstyle was probably the last thing he'd have an opinion on.

Before she could stop him, Jack had grabbed her bag and was marching towards his pickup.

"Give me that!" Amy protested, trying to wrestle it from him. "You shouldn't be carrying it. . ."

"And why not?" demanded Jack, swinging it up into the back of his pickup. "It's a lot lighter than Holly, let me tell you. Come on, get in. Lou's dying to see you."

Amy felt happiness surge through her as she clambered up into the cab. Grandpa seemed so full of energy – she hadn't seen him looking this sparkly for years. Being a great-grandfather certainly seemed to suit him.

"Holly's turned into a bundle of mischief," said Jack as he started up the engine. Heaven help us when she starts to crawl."

Amy sat back and listened as Jack described the antics of her nine-month-old niece.

"She can roll over now, which means trouble. And she's worked out this amazing technique for shuffling around on her backside. 'Shuffle-bum,' Scott calls her." Jack laughed as he pulled out on to the motorway. "You'll get a shock when you see her. Has she grown!"

It wasn't difficult to believe. To Amy, it felt like much more than five months since she'd been back. Life at college was so different, and every moment was packed. She loved the buzz of it – the excitement of having a whole new group of friends, the socializing, the stimulation of her courses and, best of all, the many different animals she got to work with. She'd stayed for a few extra days at the end of this past term to complete an extra assignment, but her first love was still horses, and she was looking forward to three whole weeks at Heartland and the opportunity to work with nothing else.

As she and Jack chatted on the drive back to the farm, Amy began to feel butterflies in her stomach. Of course, Holly would have changed – five months was a long time in the life of a baby. But what about everything else? As her grandpa steered the pickup into the long driveway, she looked eagerly at the yard. She spotted a couple of horses grazing in one of the paddocks – a chestnut gelding and a grey mare – and recognized them right away: Bear and Liberty, permanent Heartland residents who were living a happy retirement after being rescued from an auction.

Beyond another of the paddocks she saw two riders, one on a leggy chestnut gelding, and the other on her own pony, Sundance.

"That's Ty on Red!" she exclaimed, looking at Grandpa. "Is Ben here, too?" The handsome chestnut belonged to Ben Stillman, who used to work as a stable hand at Heartland. They were a talented pair – when they'd left, they'd been taken on by a top showjumping stable, and were doing really well in competitions all over the country. But Ben had kept up his contact with Heartland and always said how much his time there had helped him.

"No," Grandpa told her. "He went to stay with Tara's family in Europe and he left Red with us over Christmas."

"So we get to ride him! Fantastic." Amy watched the two horses trot up the trail. Red looked great, but Sundance was pulling as usual, fighting for his head.

"And who's that riding Sundance?" she asked.

"That's Heather," said Grandpa. "You haven't met her yet, have you?"

Amy shook her head. She and Ty had discussed finding someone to exercise Sundance because both he and Joni, the other full-time stable hand, were too heavy for him. Amy was glad for Sundance's sake that Ty had found a suitable rider, but it still felt a little weird to watch someone else ride her pony.

"Well, you will," said Grandpa. "It's great that Ty's found someone who's such a big help around the yard."

Sundance began to jog sideways, then lunged at Red's neck with his teeth bared. Amy sighed. The dun pony had always been a handful with new riders – stubborn and willful, never giving an inch. But Heather didn't seem fazed. She sat steadily in the saddle as they slowed to a walk, keeping her hands light while Sundance tossed his head and tried to whip his quarters around.

"Sundance doesn't change, does he?" she commented.

"I think you'll find that none of us change very much," said Grandpa, turning the pickup into the front yard. "Apart from Holly, that is."

Looking relaxed but a little windswept, Lou was standing outside the back door of the farmhouse, holding a small person wrapped in a cosy animal-print play suit.

With a chubby finger, the baby girl pointed at the pickup.

"Oh! There she is!" Amy exclaimed. She leaped out as the pickup came to a halt.

Jack was right. Lou looked exactly the same, but Holly . . . Amy couldn't believe her eyes. Her little niece was twice the size she'd been back in July! Then she'd been tiny, and barely able to hold her own head upright. Now, she stared out at the world with bold blue eyes – until Amy approached, that is. As Amy kissed Lou on the cheek, Holly hid her face in her mother's shoulder.

"Wow! You sure have grown!" laughed Amy. "And you've totally forgotten who I am, haven't you?"

"Don't worry," said Lou. "The shy act won't last long. Here, hold her."

Amy reached out for the rounded bundle, but Holly gave a yell of protest and clung to Lou.

"OK, OK, it's a little too soon." Lou grinned apologetically. "Honestly, make the most of it. She won't give you any peace before long. Let's get inside out of the cold."

They piled into the Heartland kitchen, and Amy luxuriated in the warm, familiar atmosphere. Lou or Grandpa's friend Nancy must have been baking, because the smell of muffins lingered on the air, along with the spicy aroma of warm apple pie.

Amy began to unwind her scarf from around her neck. "I can't believe I've been away so long," she said with a sigh.

"Neither can we," Lou agreed. She shot Amy a slightly reproachful glance. "Small animal assignment, indeed!" She had been a little hurt when Amy said she wasn't coming home right away at the end of the term.

"I know. I'm sorry. I just really wanted to finish it before coming back. Now that it's all done, I'll be able to concentrate on Christmas – and the horses."

"Don't worry. I understand. Really. I've held off on most of the Christmas stuff, so that you could help out." Lou put Holly into a bright red and yellow baby bouncer that was attached to the frame of the office door, then she fetched a pot of coffee and placed it on the table. "Freshly made," she said. "And there are muffins in the canister." She nodded at a metal container.

"You're an angel." Amy gave her sister a big hug, then sat down at the kitchen table near to Holly and smiled at her. Holly studied her carefully, an intent look in her blue eyes.

Jack dug into a muffin, and Amy joined him. "These are delicious!" she declared between mouthfuls. "I wish I could get food like this at school."

"Well, Lou made enough to feed an army. Which is a good thing – I think you made it back just before the snow," said Jack. He glanced out at the leaden-grey skies. "Looks like we're in for a storm soon."

Lou shook her head. "You've been saying that for weeks, Grandpa," she said. "You're just hoping to use some of that salt you've been hoarding."

Jack pretended to look wounded. "That salt was a bargain," he said. "And don't you forget it."

"Two tons of salt?" teased Lou. "Come on, Grandpa. We'll never get through it in a decade of winters."

"I'm heading upstairs to unpack," said Amy with a grin, swallowing the last of her coffee. "I'll let you two slug it out. You're right, Grandpa – nothing's changed around here at all!"

Amy dragged her suitcase up the stairs and made her way to her bedroom. She smiled as she pushed open the door. On her dressing table, someone – Lou or Nancy, she guessed – had placed some sprigs of holly in a little vase and wrapped silver tinsel around the base. Amy dumped her bag on her bed and flopped down beside it. She lay back and stared at the ceiling. Three whole weeks at home . . . and Christmas as well. Life at Heartland might be hard work, but it was nothing compared to the hectic pace of life at college. She was looking forward to catching up on some sleep. There had been a party pretty much every night of the week at the end of the term. Enough people had stuck around afterwards to ensure the fun continued, too. Amy couldn't remember the last time she'd got to bed before two a.m.

She sat up again and flipped open her suitcase.

"Dirty clothes, gross," she muttered, lifting them out in handfuls and shoving them into her laundry basket. At least Heartland had a washing machine. No more sitting around while the Laundromat machines munched up her money! She grinned as a memory of her classmate Will Savage popped into her mind. His kid sister had sent him a scarf supporting their local baseball team, but he'd spilled chocolate mousse all over it and threw it in with the rest of his wash – which included his white shirts, his white boxers, his white lab coat. . . What Will hadn't thought about was the colour of the scarf. It was bright red.

Amy could still picture his face when his laundry had emerged a delicate shade of pink. Poor Will. She shook her head, then she put the few clean clothes that she had into her dresser and stacked a pile of textbooks on the desk in the corner of her room. She and Will had come close to dating back in the spring when they'd done an internship together on a cattle ranch in Arizona. It had been an amazing experience, and their work with a traumatized mustang had given them a real connection. But when they got back to college, she'd still felt too close to her breakup with Ty to let anything happen. She and Will were just friends now, and Amy was happy with that. Will had started dating a friend of Amy's this term, Sharona Michaels, and Amy thought they made a great couple.

Her unpacking finished, Amy wandered over to her bedroom window. It overlooked the yard, and she opened it for a moment to lean out. Behind Grandpa's pickup, there was a little red Outback, and she spotted a petite blonde girl opening the driver's door. Amy recognized Heather, the girl who'd been riding Sundance earlier, and she craned her neck to get a better look at her. Heather raised her hand to wave at someone as she slid into the driver's seat. Amy followed the direction of her wave and saw that Ty was standing at the corner of the yard with a bridle slung over his shoulder.

Ty . . . Amy studied him. His hair was cut a bit shorter than usual, but other than that he looked the same – his lanky frame had its usual relaxed pose and, even though it was winter, his skin was tanned from constantly being outdoors. He looked just the way Amy remembered him.

Heather's car disappeared down the driveway and Ty turned away, glancing at the farmhouse as he did. Amy quickly stepped back, hoping he hadn't seen her. There were butterflies in her stomach at the thought of seeing him again. Of course, they'd chatted on the phone regularly – even though she was at college Amy wanted to be involved in the stables as much as possible – but since they'd split up, the conversations had been almost entirely about horses. They always skirted around how they were feeling about things, or what they'd been doing socially. It had sometimes felt a little awkward, especially when Amy's head was full of lectures and coursework and the latest college gossip; it could be difficult to switch back into her Heartland mode for half an hour twice a week. But now she hoped they'd be working together as closely as they had before – except that unlike the last couple of years, they weren't dating any more. How would that affect their working relationship?

Amy's friends at college had often talked about meeting up with boyfriends from their high school days. Some had said they'd been like total strangers, even though they'd only been apart for a few short months, as if separation had morphed them into totally different people. Amy hoped it wouldn't be like that with Ty, not just because they still needed to work together, but because she didn't want to lose his friendship. She had decided they should break up because it felt as if their lives were moving along different paths since she had gone away to college, but that didn't mean she had stopped appreciating him. She hoped he'd still be able to appreciate her, too, despite how much she'd moved on.

She heard a whinny from the barn and suddenly felt desperate to look around the yard and say hello to all the horses. She was bound to bump into Ty, but it would be better to get it over with; she'd have to deal with it sooner or later. Quickly, she pulled off her clean jeans and found an old working pair in her dresser. She put them on and grabbed an elastic band from her dressing table to hold back her hair, then bounded down the stairs.

"Just heading out to the yard," she said to Grandpa and Lou, who were still in the kitchen discussing feed prices. She shrugged on her barn coat and headed outside.

The air had a cold bite to it, and Amy sucked in her breath. Maybe Grandpa was right about the snow! To her surprise, the front stable block was empty – none of the stalls had horses in them. But then she noticed that the internal walls looked damp and remembered that Ty had said they'd be replastering during the quiet Christmas season. Shoving her hands into her pockets to keep them warm, she took the path that led down to the barn.

There was no sign of Ty as she pushed open the big barn door, just the familiar warm smell of horses mingled with straw, and the sound of hay nets being munched. Amy smiled when she saw that tinsel had been draped across some of the doors – where the horses couldn't reach it, of course. Red was in one of the first stalls, and Amy stopped to greet him.

"Hello, boy," she said, leaning over his half door. "You haven't forgotten me, have you?"

The big, bold chestnut had his back to her, but he turned his head when he heard her voice, his ears pricked. Amy held out her hand, inviting him to come say hello. She had missed Ben and his gorgeous horse when they moved, but she knew their talents in the jumping ring deserved special attention, more than could be fit in around the therapeutic work at Heartland.

The barn door clanked and Amy looked around, her arm still on Red's neck. Ty's form was silhouetted in the doorway. Amy swallowed, trying to suppress the butterflies that had erupted in her stomach again.

"Hi," she said.

Ty put down the water bucket he was carrying. For a moment, they regarded each other without saying anything, and Amy recognized the same nervousness on his face that she was feeling herself.

"Hi," he said. "Welcome back. Did you have a good trip?"

Amy nodded and started to move forward. Then she stopped. In the past, she would have rushed up to him for a hug, but now she stood there feeling awkward, not knowing what to do: should they shake hands or something? *Don't be ridiculous,* she told herself. But just then Ty broke the spell by walking up and touching her arm. Without pausing, he leaned forward and placed a kiss on her cheek. There was something oddly formal about it, and Amy felt a little knot tighten inside her.

Red nudged her with his muzzle, demanding attention. "I saw you riding him earlier," she said.

Ty nodded. "Ben doesn't want him getting out of shape while he's away." He smiled awkwardly. "I guess you want to look around. See who's here."

Amy nodded. "Yeah, I thought I'd better catch up," she said, keeping her voice light. She felt like a visitor; part of her wanted to remind Ty that this was her home as well as the place where he worked, but then she told herself that the awkwardness came just as much from her as from him. If she couldn't cope with Ty on a personal level, she'd have to focus on their strong professional relationship to get them through this tricky moment.

Ty picked up his water bucket again, and Amy followed him. "Looks like the barn's full," she commented as they walked past some of the stalls.

Ty nodded. "Nearly all residents, though," he said. "Even though we might not get the Arctic conditions Jack's been forecasting for the last couple of weeks, it's still warmer in here than in the paddocks." He stopped outside the stall of an elderly bay mare and let himself in. "Shalom kicked her bucket over earlier. Girl's getting clumsy in her old age."

Amy smiled briefly, and stroked Shalom's nose. The mare had been rescued from an overcrowded, overheated cattle truck, along with four other horses. Some of the others in the truck had not been so fortunate and had died of shock and thirst. It had been one of the most traumatic experiences of Amy's life, but she had got through it with Ty's support and understanding. He always seemed to know when to soothe her and when to let her vent her emotions, and he had been more than patient in letting her express all the grief and anger she felt at the way those horses had been treated.

Ty let himself out of the stall again, his whole body tensing as he brushed close to Amy. *I can't believe this,* she thought. *Manoeuvring around each other like we just met.* Even the way they were chatting about the horses was stilted, like making small talk at a party. It hadn't been this difficult to talk on the phone. Why was it so much harder face-to-face?

"Tara left Apollo here, too," Ty informed her as they continued down the barn. "It made sense for her and Ben to stable their horses together while they're away in Europe."

"I'd be happy to ride either of them, if you need me to," Amy offered.

If you need me to. The last phrase slipped out and she knew it said everything: the truth was, Amy and Ty used to make all their decisions together. Now it felt like she was deliberately stepping back to let Ty take charge – as if the fact they'd stopped dating meant they couldn't work as equals any more.

They reached Apollo's stall and Amy said hello to the striking pure-grey show jumper. Her mind was whirling, full of the voices of her college friends talking about their former boyfriends. *It's so weird, how they become strangers . . . like that was a totally different life . . . a totally different person. . .*

The thought that Ty could feel like a stranger had seemed a crazy idea to Amy back then. But right now she understood exactly what they'd meant.

Chapter Two

A high-pitched whinny broke into Amy's thoughts and she looked down towards the end of the barn. "Who's that?"

"It's the only visitor in here for treatment at the moment," said Ty. "Flamenco."

"What's wrong with her?" Amy asked as they approached the stall. She gazed over the half door at a gorgeous bright chestnut mare, who stared back at Amy with her neck arched. Her legs and shoulders were held taut, ready to spring away in an instant, but all the same, her ears were pricked as if she was curious about her visitors. Amy held her breath. She was beautiful.

"There's nothing *wrong* with her exactly," said Ty. "Treatment's not quite the word, I guess. The trouble is, she's already six. She was backed last year, but her owners are still finding her too much of a handful. So they want her to go through the backing process again."

Amy gazed at the mare's long, flowing mane and broad, dished face. "Looks like she's got some Andalusian in her," she commented.

"Not just some," said Ty. "She's purebred, apparently."

Slowly, Amy offered her hand for the mare to sniff

before reaching towards her smooth, copper-coloured neck. Flamenco rolled her eyes, then lunged forward and gave Amy a sharp nip on her arm.

"Ow!" she exclaimed, jumping back. "She's quite a character, isn't she?"

For the first time, Ty gave a genuine grin. "Yeah. I think that's an understatement."

Amy could tell from the mare's big, luscious eyes and pricked ears that there was nothing really malicious about her. She was just full of life and energy. "Is she always kept in?"

"Most of the time, from what the owners said," said Ty. "I'm planning on turning her out, but she only arrived yesterday so I'm giving her a day or so in the barn to settle in."

Amy nodded. Six years old was late to be going through the backing process; it wouldn't be easy for her to submit to a rider now. She didn't blame Flamenco for wanting to stay wild a little longer. "What are her owners like?"

"Oh, they're devoted to her," said Ty. "They're a young couple, Julia and Rick Breakspear. Flamenco is Julia's really, but they're both involved. You could meet them, if you want to – they're coming over tomorrow to see how she's doing."

"Tomorrow!" Amy was astonished. "They're not expecting to see any change by then, are they?"

"No, no," Ty said hurriedly. "They know it could take a while. In fact, they say they're happy for her to stay for as long as it takes. They're not expecting miracles. They want to maintain their relationship with her, that's all."

"That's a good sign."

Ty nodded. "Yes. They obviously want the best for her – they're just not sure how to give it."

As well as Red, Shalom, Apollo and Flamenco, one other horse was in his stall, and that was the old Heartland resident Jake. Amy greeted him affectionately, and he whinnied a welcome.

"He's pretty stiff these days," said Ty. "His arthritis is so bad, it doesn't seem fair to put him out. The paddocks are very hard underfoot after the frosts. That's why Shalom's in, too – the ground's too much for her navicular."

As Amy patted the old gelding's nose, a thought occurred to her. "We had a horse with navicular at the college yard," she said. "He hated being kept in so we put him in one of the school rings with a pile of hay. The sand's a bit gentler on painful joints."

"I hadn't thought of that," Ty said. "Good idea."

Amy threw him a quick glance. She hoped he didn't

mind her making suggestions; she had no intention of making him think that she was going to take over just because she was home for vacation. Some of the awkwardness between them had begun to ebb away as they'd talked about Flamenco, but she wasn't sure what had taken its place. Ty didn't seem at all put out by her suggestion; instead, he seemed . . . well, pleased to hear what she had to say. Amy told herself to stop overanalyzing everything. They were two adults having a grown-up conversation, politely and reasonably, about a professional matter. For some reason, the thought was kind of depressing.

They headed out of the barn and to the paddocks. On the way, Amy realized she hadn't seen Joni, their full-time Canadian stable hand.

"Is Joni away?" she asked.

Ty nodded. "She left three days ago. She won't be back until the New Year. But she made sure she put some tinsel up before she left."

Amy smiled, thinking of the decorations in the barn. "I guess she went to Alberta?"

"Yeah. Her mom is hosting a big family gathering over the holidays."

They reached the first paddock, and Ty leaned on

the gate, clicking his tongue at the horses. Libby and Bear raised their heads from grazing, then began to amble over. Sundance was in the same paddock. He looked up, but just swished his tail and carried on grazing. Amy smiled. Her feisty pony was way too proud to come over right away.

"I saw someone with you out on the trail earlier," she said. "A girl riding Sundance. Grandpa said she's helping out on the yard. I think he said her name's Heather, is that right?"

"Yeah." Ty held out a handful of pony nuts for Bear to lip off his fingers.

"How did you find her? Did you advertise?"

Ty looked surprised. "No, nothing like that. She saw Joni and me out riding one day and asked if we had any horses that needed exercising."

"Well, she's a good rider," said Amy. She wanted to make sure Ty knew she was fine with having someone else ride her pony. Another time, she might have been tempted to tell Ty how strange it was at first to see someone else riding Sundance, but not today. "I thought she was handling Sundance well."

Ty smiled. "Heather's a natural. She hasn't had much formal training, but she isn't fazed by all his messing around."

Sundance had stopped grazing and was watching the other two horses chewing on pony nuts at the gate. He looked torn between keeping his distance and getting in on the treats. "You'll have missed out on everything in a minute!" she called to him.

Ty brushed his hands together before putting them back in his pockets. "He's too late already," he said. "I need the rest of the nuts to catch Aria. I'm planning on riding her out this afternoon."

"Oh." Amy wasn't sure how to respond. She'd love to go out on the trails, too, but it felt as if she needed to check that it would be OK with Ty. Sundance had already been out, so had Red. She was dying to see Spindleberry, the horse she'd adopted as her own from the ones rescued from the truck, but although the three-year-old had been backed, she didn't know how far he'd got in his training. "Well, I'll come with you to the bottom paddock. I guess Spindle's there, too?"

"Yes. And Jasmine and Nickel. You know about Nickel?"

"Holly's Shetland pony? Yes, Lou told me about him on the phone. Apparently he's the image of Sugarfoot." Sugarfoot was a tufty chestnut Shetland who had almost given up on life after his elderly owner died, but was nursed back to health by Lou who developed a special connection with him.

They reached the paddock gate and Ty opened it for them both to pass through. Jasmine and Aria looked up as they entered. Jasmine, a pretty black mare with a dished Arabian face, whickered a greeting, then continued to graze. Amy looked up to the far corner of the paddock for Spindle. The handsome dark roan was there, but he hadn't spotted her yet.

Her mouth dry with anticipation, she called. "Spindle!"

Spindle's head jerked up. He stood stock-still for an instant, his ears pricked. Then he turned towards the gate, his tail held high, and broke into a canter. Amy felt her heart swell with pride and delight. *He still recognizes me!* She glanced quickly at Ty, wanting to share her pleasure, but he was watching Spindle, too.

Even with his warm New Zealand rug on, Amy could tell that Spindle was in good health and that his muscles had developed further since she'd last seen him. His neck and haunches looked a little bit more defined and powerful; at three years old, he was pretty much fully grown, but he would continue to develop more strength for a while.

Amy flung her arms around his neck and hugged him.

"Spindle! You remember me!" she exclaimed. "Good boy."

"I'll get Aria while you two get acquainted again," Ty said, and walked off towards the black mare who was studying the reunion from the other side of the field.

Amy reached up to straighten Spindle's forelock, laughing as he butted her with his soft muzzle. She adored his curious, playful spirit, and the courage with which he had put his terrible experience in the overheated cattle truck behind him.

"There's something I was going to suggest," said Ty as he led Aria back across the paddock. "I didn't know if you'd be up for riding today, since you just got here. . ."

Amy looked at him, incredulous. How could he think that she might *not* want to ride? "Are you crazy?"

Ty gave an awkward shrug. "Well, you could be tired from travelling or something."

Amy knew her eyes were flashing, and she looked away. There was no reason to get angry with Ty when he had been trying to think of what might be best for her. She calmed herself, and looked up more gently. "I'd love to ride, if there's a horse that needs exercising."

"Actually I was going to suggest you ride Spindle. He's been doing really well in the school, but Joni and I thought you might like to be the first one to take him out on the trail."

Amy stared at him. "Really?"

"We can take him out now, if you want to." Ty opened the gate and led Aria out.

Amy grinned. This was by far the best thing she could have hoped to do on her first afternoon at home. "You bet!" she exclaimed.

Ty smiled back. "Glad you're up for it," he said, and began to lead Aria up to the yard.

As Amy followed with Spindle, using a halter that had been hanging on a fence post by the gate, she really felt like she was home.

"Getting right back to work, I see," Jack teased, striding across the yard as Amy emerged from the tack room with Spindle's saddle and bridle.

"I'm taking Spindle out," she explained happily.

"Good for you. You'll need to make the most of the dry weather," said Jack, glancing up at the sky. "There might not be much more of it."

"Is that the prophet of doom I hear again?" called Ty from the other side of the yard. "You've been predicting snow for . . . how long, Jack? Three weeks?"

Jack shook his head. "You might mock," he said. "But

it's not far off, mark my words." He raised his hand in a wave and headed towards the barn. "Have a good ride!"

It was nice to hear Ty sounding more relaxed, and Amy smiled at him as she slipped Spindle's saddle on to his back. "Sounds like Grandpa's got a bee in his bonnet about snow," she commented. "Lou figures it's because he wants to use some of his salt."

Ty laughed. "Yeah, we've been teasing him about that all week."

"You don't think he's right, then?" she asked. "About the weather, I mean."

"Well, it's winter," said Ty matter-of-factly. "It's bound to snow at some point."

He waited while Amy finished tacking up. Spindleberry stood quietly as she slipped the headband over his ears and did up the noseband and throatlash. He opened his mouth to accept the gentle snaffle bit, and played with it between his teeth as she tightened the girth.

"All right, boy, you're ready," she murmured, feeling her stomach flip over in anticipation as she swung herself into the saddle. She loved helping young horses achieve their first milestones – working on the lunge, being backed, heading out on to the trails – but with Spindle it felt even more special because she'd been involved in his training right from the start, and because he was hers.

Ty mounted Aria and nudged her forward. "I was thinking we could go along Clairdale Ridge," he said over his shoulder. "I told you about the new lumberyard, right? The one owned by the Middletons?"

"I don't think you mentioned it, no. Does that mean there's lots of logging going on?"

"Kind of," said Ty. "They're pretty busy. Let's go. I'll show you where it is."

Spindle's ears were pricked and, as they took a path away from the school rings and out on to the trail, Amy could feel his excitement. He pranced a little, straining to keep up with Aria, his hooves dancing on the frozen ground. Amy sat still and light in the saddle, keeping a gentle contact on the reins. Her heart warmed as the young roan horse responded to her, listening to her as she soothed him with her voice.

They kept a slow pace for a while, following the trail as it led away from Heartland, then trotted under the pine trees alongside the forest. Amy let Spindle find his own balance at the faster pace; since his neck muscles were still undeveloped, this meant his head wasn't held perpendicular to the ground like a highly schooled horse, but was stretched forward a little. Amy wouldn't start to encourage him into a tighter outline until next year, when his hindquarters would be stronger.

As the trail took them up towards the ridge, Amy heard the whine of buzz saws.

Ty brought Aria back to a walk and turned in his saddle. "The Middletons' yard is up ahead," he said. "I guess it'll be a bit of a test for Spindle. Do you want to come alongside?"

"Thanks," she said, riding Spindle forward. "He feels pretty calm. You and Joni have been doing a great job with him."

Ty looked pleased and flashed her a smile. The rasp and whine of the saws got louder and Spindle began to balk. Amy shortened her reins and closed her legs on his sides to reassure him.

"It's OK," she murmured. "Nothing to worry about. Easy does it, Spindle."

The young horse inched closer to Aria, instinctively wanting to be close to the steady, experienced mare. They continued on, Amy's leg almost brushing Ty's. She was acutely aware of how close he was, but she kept her mind focused on the young horse underneath her. In a clear demonstration of his trust, Spindle obeyed the gentle pressure from Amy's calf muscles telling him to ignore his instincts and keep moving towards the unfamiliar noises.

"He's doing really well," said Ty. Amy nodded, pleased that Ty was here to share another important step in Spindle's training.

The blue roofs of the lumberyard were just coming into view when he indicated a trail off to the left. "We can turn down here," he suggested. "It'll take us on a little detour away from the worst of the noise."

As the whir of the saws began to fade, Spindle's muscles relaxed and Amy loosened the reins, patting his neck to praise him for staying so calm. They trotted again as the path wound down through the trees and out alongside a field. Spindle and Aria noticed the field's occupants before Amy did, and Spindle gave a high-pitched whinny.

"Oh, *look*!" Amy exclaimed, gazing into the field. A grey mare about fifteen hands high and a nut-brown donkey were grazing a little way from the fence. She reined in Spindle. "What a cute donkey!"

The donkey stuck its nose into the air and brayed, its squeaky voice sounding almost painful, then trotted up to get a better look at the two horses. Spindle peered over the fence, his ears pricked in fascination.

The mare looked up but stayed where she was. She was pretty enough to be a show horse with her pale dappled-stone-coloured coat and flowing white mane. At first glance she looked very overweight, but Amy quickly realized what the bulging stomach and flattened back meant. The mare was heavily pregnant, and Amy tried to recall what she'd learned at college to gauge how long it would be before she gave birth.

"Looks like she's only got a few weeks to go," she told Ty. "If that."

"D'you think so?" Ty looked over at the mare. "I guess you're right. She's pretty big, and you're the vet. You should know!"

His voice was warm with the teasing tone that Amy knew so well, and she laughed. "Not yet, I'm not," she said. "Only another five years to go!"

"No time at all," said Ty. "You'll be back here running Heartland before you know it."

Amy wasn't sure how to respond. What was Ty trying to say? It sounded like he was suggesting that life hadn't changed all that much – in the long run, they would both end up working together the way they always had. Amy wasn't so sure but, all the same, she was surprised to feel her stomach give a little flip. "Well, I hope all the work will be worth it, wherever I end up," she said guardedly. She studied the mare again. The pregnant horse looked in good health and had her full winter coat. "The donkey's good company for her," Amy commented. "He won't get jealous of the foal, either, the way another horse might."

"Lungworm could be a problem, though, couldn't it?" asked Ty, turning Aria on to the trail again.

Amy nodded. Donkeys could transmit the worms to horses that lived in the same field, giving them a nasty hacking cough. "It's easily avoided," she said. "You just have to worm them both regularly. But those two look in good condition."

Spindle trotted after Aria, his stride swinging out smoothly. As the horses climbed the track that rose back up to the ridge, Amy called to Ty. "We could canter here, just up to the top?"

"If you're sure," he responded, looking back over his shoulder.

Amy nodded. "I think it'd be good for him."

Aria set a steady pace and Spindle bounded after her eagerly, breaking into an excited sweat as they started up the slope. Amy held him back and his stride steadied, then slowed as they climbed the steepest part of the slope.

"Good boy," Amy praised him, bringing him back to a trot as they rejoined the main trail. "You're learning fast."

They followed the trail in a loop back towards Heartland.

The afternoon was starting to darken and thick purple shadows were spreading over the ridge. Amy began to feel cold. All the same, she was glowing inside at how well Spindle had done, and she was delighted that Ty and Joni had been so thoughtful about waiting for her to give him his first ride on a trail.

"Thanks, Ty," she said, once they were untacking the horses. "It was great of you to think of me. About Spindle, I mean."

"A pleasure," he said, hooking Aria's saddle over his arm. He grinned at her, making the corners of his eyes crinkle. "It's good to have you back on the yard. I hope you haven't forgotten how to muck out?"

"No problem! Everything at Heartland's feels like a holiday compared to college."

"I don't believe you for one–"

Suddenly, the farmhouse door flew open and Nancy Marshall ran out. "Amy!" she cried, enveloping her in a hug. "It's so lovely to see you. I can't believe you've been out riding already. You just got here!"

Amy laughed, kissing the older woman on both cheeks. Nancy had been part of her grandpa's life for a while now and felt as much part of the family as Lou's husband, Scott. "It's great to see you, too, Nancy. And I'm sorry – I just couldn't resist."

"Well, I hope you worked up an appetite," said Nancy. "I brought a casserole over for us all to share. Lou took Holly home, so it's just the three of us – unless you'd like to stay, Ty? There's plenty."

Amy looked at Ty. The trail ride had made things feel much more relaxed and easy between them, and it would be great to spend an evening with him so they could really catch up. But Ty shook his head. "Sorry, Nancy," he said. "I know how good your casseroles are, but I've got other plans, I'm afraid. Jack said he'd cover the evening chores."

Swallowing her disappointment, Amy put Spindle's tack away, then helped Ty take in the rest of the horses. When they were all safely in their stalls in the barn, she accompanied him to his pickup to see him off.

"I want to start work with Flamenco tomorrow," he said, opening the driver's door. "Would you be up for that?"

"Of course," Amy said. "Just try to stop me."

Ty grinned. "I knew it wouldn't take you too long to settle back in," he said. "See you in the morning."

Chapter Three

Once Ty was gone, Amy went back down to the barn. The warmth of twelve horses greeted her and contrasted with the biting cold air outside as she opened the door. She walked down the aisle, checking that they were all comfortable. Ty was right – it hadn't taken her long to settle back in; she was relieved that the ice between them was starting to thaw.

"Did you have a good ride this afternoon?" Jack asked her, scooping out oats from a big feed bin.

"Great," said Amy. "Spindle's doing so well. I can hardly believe how far he's come."

Jack nodded. "Ty and Joni have both been working really hard," he said. "In fact, I don't know what we'd do without Ty. He holds the place together these days, lucky for us."

Amy realized Jack was right: They *were* lucky. It hadn't occurred to her before, but Ty could easily have made some changes or tried to impose his own ideas on the routines at Heartland – even subtle shifts would have made a difference. But he hadn't. He had always believed in the methods that Amy's mother, Marion, had taught him, and he kept the spirit of Heartland true to what she would have wanted.

"I'm glad, Grandpa," she said. "But I guess it must be lonely for you, now that you have the farmhouse all to yourself."

"Don't you worry about me, honey. I'm fine. Lou and Holly are here all the time, and they often stay for dinner – Scott joins us here when he finishes work. And I see plenty of Nancy. She's always got some plan or other for filling my time." Grandpa paused, his blue eyes looking reflective. For a moment, Amy thought he was about to say something else, but then he shook his head and carried on with the feeds.

The work was soon done. Closing the barn door on the quietly feeding horses, Amy looked up to the warm glow of light from the farmhouse window. She sighed happily. It was definitely good to be back.

To her surprise, Amy woke up early the next morning – much earlier than she usually did at college. Jumping out of bed seemed easy when there wasn't a lecture or a paper that needed to be finished waiting for her. She threw on her work clothes and headed outside into a cold, crisp morning. Ty hadn't arrived yet, so she got started on the morning feeds. She worked methodically, greeting all the horses and chatting away with each of them as she brought them their breakfast. Once they'd finished eating she led Jake and Shalom out into the pale morning light and up to the smaller school ring. Shalom trotted around on the soft sand with her tail kinked, and even old Jake seemed brighter. Amy got them a pile of hay then turned out the rest of the horses, leaving just Apollo, Red, and Flamenco in their stalls, before making a start on the mucking out. She'd already done four stalls when she heard Ty's pickup pull up.

Ty whistled when he saw how much work Amy had done. "Hey!" he exclaimed. "Looks like I'll be able to sleep in a bit while you're around."

"Don't count on it," said Amy. "This is my first day. Give me a week and you'll have to drag me out of bed."

"OK. OK. I'll just make the most of it while it lasts."

Together, they finished off the mucking out, then Amy got a halter from the tack room so that they could start work with Flamenco.

"I was going to work her loose in the school, just to get a feel for her," said Ty. "But maybe you'd like to do it? I could check over the feed bins instead."

"Sure," said Amy. She felt secretly pleased that she'd

get a chance to work with the spirited Andalusian on her own for a while. She'd sensed a connection with the mare's wild spirit the day before and a moment of sympathy for her resistance to any sort of formal training. "I'd say the main thing is to establish join-up as quickly as possible. She needs to trust us before we do anything else."

Ty nodded. "Yeah, I agree. Join-up should be quite an experience for her – I get the feeling she's never gone through it before."

Amy headed to the bottom of the barn and let herself into the mare's stall. Flamenco rolled her eyes at Amy and wouldn't lower her head for the halter at first. Amy took her time, talking to the mare soothingly and letting her get used to her presence in the stall. After a while Flamenco began to relax and allowed Amy to slip the halter over her ears.

"Good girl," Amy praised her. "I'm not so bad after all, am I?"

She led the chestnut out of her stall and down the aisle of the barn. Flamenco danced and spooked all the way, calling out to Red and Apollo in high-pitched whinnies. She was insatiably curious about the other horses, so Amy allowed her to take a good look at them.

"Now, come on," said Amy, once Flamenco had said

hello. "You've got work to do."

The mare resisted, throwing up her head and flattening her ears. "That's enough," Amy chided her without raising her voice. "Is this how you behave at home?" She kept level with Flamenco's shoulder, knowing that horses felt threatened by someone directly in front of them, and clicked her tongue to make her walk on. With a toss of her head, Flamenco stepped elegantly down the aisle as if it had been her idea all along.

She decided to give the mare a quick brush over before taking her up to the school. Rather than tying her to the metal ring in the grooming area, Amy clipped a lunge line to Flamenco's headcollar in place of the lead rope and ran it through the ring, looping the spare line in her left hand. That way, if Flamenco ran back, Amy could release her immediately so that she didn't pull against the ring and hurt herself. Sure enough, Flamenco fidgeted as Amy began work, her muscles taut. Being kept cooped up in the barn all day was clearly difficult for her – she was so full of life, and she seemed desperate to let off some steam.

"Don't worry, girl, I'll be quick," said Amy, soothing her with long, firm strokes of the body brush. "I can tell you want to get started."

She was just finishing up when she heard the sound of a

car arriving in the front yard. She wondered who it might be. Surely not the Breakspears already? But when Ty appeared around the side of the stable block with a couple by his side, she guessed it must be them after all. Amy was slightly disappointed. She had hoped to do some work with Flamenco before speaking to them – now they would want to watch, which might distract Flamenco. But it would be interesting to see how they reacted to Flamenco's first session.

"Amy, this is Rick and Julia Breakspear," said Ty. He turned to them. "And this is Amy Fleming. It was Amy's mother, Marion, who started Heartland."

Still holding the end of the lunge line, Amy shook hands, first with Julia and then with Rick. They were both tall and wiry. Rick didn't look particularly outdoorsy; he had a bookish, earnest air. Julia, on the other hand, had the tanned, weatherbeaten skin of someone who spent most of her life in the open.

"Great to meet you, Amy," she said. "Ty tells me we're just in time to see Flamenco's first training session."

Amy nodded. "That's right. She's all ready to go." She stepped back to let Julia greet her horse, who was watching with her nostrils flared.

Julia's face broke into a beaming smile. "There's my

girl!" she murmured. Amy exchanged glances with Ty, and he gave a little smile. One thing was clear – Julia loved her horse to pieces, which had to be a good start.

Flamenco whinnied a greeting, shifting her hooves so that they clattered on the stone floor. Julia moved to stand in front her, her expression stern. "Now you stand nicely for me," she told the mare. Flamenco butted her with her nose. "No, that's not nice. You don't do that," she said, her voice firm. "Stand still."

Amy watched, interested, then turned to Rick. "Is this Julia's first horse?" she asked.

Rick looked astonished and shook his head. "No, no. She's had horses for the last fifteen years. In fact, we've still got Logris."

"Logris?" From the way Rick said his name, it sounded as though he expected Amy to know who he was.

"Her top-flight dressage horse. She trained him herself and competed on him for the last decade or so. We just retired him. Julia's hoping that Flamenco will carry the torch now – if she'll respond to her training, that is."

Julia turned her attention away from Flamenco for a moment. "What's that about Logris?"

"I was just explaining how you had to retire him," said Rick.

"Yes," said Julia. "Logris is wonderful, but he's getting so old and stiff, poor boy."

"So you're hoping that Flamenco will be a successful dressage horse, too?" asked Amy.

Julia nodded. "Yes. Flamenco should be one of the best. Her father's Belmiro, the famous Andalusian show stallion." She looked at her horse proudly, then laid a hand on her neck as she talked. "With a lineage like that, she's a real challenge. Belmiro has a reputation for being fiery and willful. But I hope you can see what I'm aiming for – all her fire and beauty contained within the discipline of dressage. She'll be amazing."

Looking at Flamenco's showy crest and powerful haunches, Amy could see that perfectly well. "I hope we'll be able to help," she said.

The mare was growing impatient, scraping her hooves on the ground.

"I think we should get her up to the arena," said Ty. He went to get the lead rope that was hanging close by, but Julia reached for it herself.

"She gets so excited," she said. "Maybe it's best if I lead her up there for you."

Amy and Ty exchanged glances. They both knew from long experience that it could be hard for owners to let go and accept that other people knew how to handle their horses – even when they had sent them to Heartland for that purpose. But it was important for Julia to feel relaxed about leaving her horse in their hands. "That's fine," said Amy. "It's this way."

Julia took her time, talking constantly to Flamenco as she attached the lead rope to the halter and unclipped the lunge line, which Amy coiled up to take down to the school. Clicking to encourage Flamenco to move away from the grooming area, Julia began to follow Ty and Amy down the track. "Steady now," she warned the mare. "Pick your feet up. Good girl. Let's stay calm, OK?"

Flamenco peered up the track, ears pricked. She wanted to know what lay ahead. Amy saw a sheen of sweat on her neck, a sure sign of excitement – and it was no wonder why. She'd been kept indoors for a couple of days, and this was a whole new environment. When she began to jog sideways, Julia stopped her.

"Hey. We're not going anywhere until you calm down," she told the mare in a firm tone. After resisting for a while, Flamenco dropped her head and stood still for a few seconds. Julia praised her, then led her on again. It seemed a little bit over the top. Flamenco was a fiery horse in new surroundings – she was bound to want a good look around.

She wasn't misbehaving, or at least not intentionally.

As they neared the two schools, Julia looked alarmed. "Oh! There are horses here," she exclaimed, seeing Jake and Shalom in the smaller ring.

"Don't worry, we'll use the other school," said Amy.

"Yes, but they're a bit of a distraction, aren't they?" said Julia. She looked over towards the paddocks where the other horses were. "Isn't there an indoor school where we could work her?"

Amy was surprised. "But you want to compete with her, don't you?" she asked. "She'll need to get used to working around other horses." She took in Julia's anxious expression and realized she needed to be reassured. "Jake and Shalom are both very quiet," she promised. "I'm sure we'll be able to get Flamenco to concentrate."

They reached the school gate and, rather reluctantly, Julia handed the lead rope to Amy. Amy led the mare into the centre of the school and went to unclip the lead rope, but a call from Julia stopped her.

"Please don't unclip her," she called. "She's much too wound up at the moment, especially with these other horses nearby. I always began a session with Logris by lunging him. I found it really helped his concentration. Could do you that instead?"

Amy paused, her hand still on the clip, trying not to feel too frustrated. Julia could see perfectly well that Flamenco wasn't wearing a lunging cavesson. The lunge line in Amy's hand would be used to keep Flamenco going during the join-up. She looked over at Ty, wondering if he felt equally frustrated. He gave a little shrug that neither Rick nor Julia could see. Amy guessed what he meant. It wouldn't help to stand around arguing, and it was good to get a picture of how Julia liked to work.

"That's fine. I'll go and grab a cavesson," Ty said. He smiled at Julia. "Maybe you'd like to lead Flamenco around while you're waiting?"

A look of relief passed over Julia's face, and she hurried into the centre of the ring and took the lead rope back from Amy. Amy wandered back over to Rick, who stood watching from the gate, his expression serious.

"I sure hope you'll be able to help us," he said. "She's one firecracker of a mare."

"Well, she's lively," Amy agreed. "But that's nothing to worry about in and of itself. We've worked with horses that were much more difficult than Flamenco."

"You have?" Rick's eyebrows shot up, as though he found it hard to imagine how a horse could be any more difficult. "Well, that's good to hear."

Ty jogged back from the yard with the lunging cavesson and whip, and Julia led Flamenco back to the gate. Expertly, Ty fitted the bitless bridle on to the mare and stepped back, giving Amy a quick smile. "All yours," he said.

Amy led Flamenco back into the centre of the ring and sent her out in a circle on the end of the lunge line. With all the waiting, Flamenco had gotten even more restless, so Amy decided to skip walking and move her straight into a trot. She gave a playful kick of her heels before setting off, then circled Amy at a fast, ragged trot, breaking into a canter every few strides. Amy kept her going forward. She wasn't worried about the mare's exuberance – she knew it would take a while for her to calm down. But after a couple of circuits, a gust of wind buffeted the mare's mane and she wheeled around on her hindquarters, giving an excited whinny.

It was too much for Julia. She left the gate and hurried to Flamenco's head. "I'll lead her," she said to Amy. "She's getting much too worked up. She'll hurt herself if she carries on like this!"

Amy lowered the lunging whip as Ty followed Julia across the school. "Really, Flamenco will be fine," he said. "We won't let anything happen to her."

Julia's jaw jutted. "I think I know my own horse," she snapped. "She easily gets out of hand. In fact, I don't know why you haven't put her in lunging reins to keep her head in the correct position."

Amy gathered up the lunge line and walked over. "We prefer to school horses in a more natural shape to start with," she explained. Lunge reins were elasticated reins that ran from the horse's bit to a surcingle or girth; they held the horse's head down and encouraged them to power forward from their hindquarters. But like Spindle, Flamenco's muscles weren't yet developed enough to cope with working in a tight outline, so lunge reins would just make her feel tied down and restricted.

Julia looked from Ty to Amy and back again, her mouth clamped shut. She glanced over to Rick who still stood at the gateway, appealing to him with her eyes.

"Maybe these people are right, honey," he called. "We have to trust them if we're going to leave Flamenco here."

Julia hesitated, and suddenly Amy felt sorry for her. It was clear that she was genuinely concerned about her horse and was struggling with herself over choosing the best course of action. It must have been a difficult decision to send the mare to Heartland: After all, Julia was an experienced and successful rider. Her competition record with Logris was ample evidence of that. Her standards were high, and it couldn't have been easy to admit she couldn't fix things on her own.

At last, Julia let go of Flamenco's bridle and walked slowly back to the gate. Ty walked back with her and Amy started work again with the mare, changing the rein and trotting her in the opposite direction.

Flamenco danced and tossed her head around, refusing to listen to Amy's commands. Amy made the lunge circle smaller and kept her going, ignoring the way Flamenco was contorting her neck. She knew the smaller circle would make it difficult for the mare to sustain her balance in a canter, and, sure enough, she soon began to stay at a trot. Once she had used up some of her energy, Amy worked on transitions, down to a walk and back into a trot, until at last the fiery chestnut lowered her head and her trot became more measured.

Aware that it had all been quite a lot for the young horse to handle, Amy decided to keep the session short and end on a positive note. She brought Flamenco to a halt and led her over to the gate.

Julia looked relieved and produced a horse cookie from her pocket. "Well, that wasn't so bad," she acknowledged, feeding Flamenco the cookie. "Will you work her again later?"

"No, not today," Amy replied. "That's enough for her to start with. We need to give her time to settle down and get used to her surroundings before we introduce totally new ideas to her schooling. She did really well in her first session, though – I think she'll progress very quickly. It would be good to reward her with some freedom out in the paddock now."

"The paddock?" Julia looked alarmed. "But there are other horses there."

There was a pause. Amy wasn't sure how to respond. Julia's approach to Flamenco was totally at odds with how she'd handle the mare herself, but it was obviously a style that might work well with a calmer, less demanding horse. "That shouldn't be a problem," she said eventually. "Doesn't she ever graze with Logris?"

"Not on her own. I hand-graze her sometimes, on a lead rein. I think she's just too highly strung to deal with more than that."

"We could put her in our small paddock, behind the barn," suggested Ty. "It's empty at the moment. She'll be perfectly safe on her own."

Amy nodded. It was a good compromise.

"Well . . . I guess that would be OK," said Julia. Still

looking doubtful, she and Rick followed as Amy led the chestnut mare down past the main paddocks to the little one behind the barn and opened the gate. Flamenco suddenly understood that she was going to be let loose and her limbs trembled with excitement as Amy undid the buckles on the cavesson. Ty helped to hold her steady until Amy could slip it over her head, and then the mare was away, cantering across the grass and throwing her heels up in a couple of lighthearted bucks. She looked stunning with the winter sun catching her golden-red coat, and Amy glanced at Julia, expecting her to be full of pride in her beautiful horse.

But she wasn't. Instead, Julia was gripping the gate, her knuckles white as she stared at Flamenco's antics. Rick was holding her arm, supporting her.

Amy thought quickly. She knew words of reassurance wouldn't work here; Julia needed to see for herself that Flamenco wasn't going to get hurt by letting off some steam. "I'll get some hay," she said. "That'll encourage her to graze. There's not a lot of grass out there at this time of year."

Ty caught her eye and nodded. "Don't worry, I'll go," he said, and jogged off around the barn. He was back in a few moments with a quarter-bale of hay, and let himself through the gate. Flamenco watched him shake out the hay for her, curious, then wheeled on her haunches and did a few more circuits of the paddock. Ty walked away, leaving the mare to investigate the hay in her own time.

It was a few more moments before Flamenco approached the hay. She sniffed it, then snatched a mouthful, lifting her head at once to look at her audience.

"There," said Amy. "She'll be fine now. I think we should leave her to it."

"We can't just–" Julia began, but then Amy saw Rick put a hand on her arm, and she stopped with a sigh. "OK. If that's what you think is best."

They all walked slowly back to the yard. Rick made polite comments about the facilities while Julia seemed lost in thought.

"I'm sure you can see the problem we have with Flamenco," she said finally as the Breakspears reached their car. "It's so difficult to connect with her. She's so distracted all the time. I hope you'll help us find a way to reach her."

"Well, she's got spirit," Amy agreed. She smiled. "I can see how much you care about her, and knowing you're on her side will make it a lot easier for her to make some changes."

Julia opened the door of the car, but paused for a moment before getting in. "You will let me know if anything goes wrong, won't you?"

"Of course," Amy promised. "But I don't think it will. She'll settle down in a couple of days."

Julia took a deep breath, then lowered herself into the seat. "OK. Well – thank you, Amy. It's been good to meet you."

"And you, too," said Amy.

She and Ty stood side by side as the couple fastened their seat belts and drove off down the drive. It was only when the car had finally disappeared that Amy let her shoulders relax. Without realizing it, she'd been clenching them. "Hmm. Interesting," she said.

Ty nodded. "Something tells me we have more than one problem."

"Yeah," Amy agreed. "There's plenty of work to do with Flamenco – she's not going to accept a rider without challenging the boundaries, that's clear. But Julia sure brings some tension into the equation. I can still feel it now."

Ty gave a wry smile. "And if we're picking up on it after one session, imagine what Flamenco must feel."

Chapter Four

Amy went into the farmhouse to grab a snack – between starting early and the Breakspears arriving, she'd completely forgotten about breakfast. She found Nancy sitting at the kitchen table, flipping through the mail to the sound of Christmas carols on the radio.

"Hi, Nancy," Amy greeted her, heading for the basket of muffins that sat near the fridge. To her disappointment, it was empty. "Are we out of muffins?"

Nancy looked up, surprised. "Out of muffins? Oh . . ." She frowned. "I'm sorry, Amy. I'll bake some this afternoon. There's plenty of bread, isn't there?"

Amy looked in the bread box. "Plenty. I'll make toast instead. Thanks, Nancy. Where's Lou this morning?"

"She took Holly to their mom and baby group," said Nancy. She opened an envelope and pulled out a card. "Lou made some wonderful friends there."

"I guess she needs people to talk diapers with." Amy put a couple of slices of bread into the toaster and sat down at the table. She watched as Nancy made a note of who had sent the Christmas cards, then gathered together a pile of empty envelopes. "Anything interesting in the mail today?"

"Lots of Christmas cards."

Amy stood up as the toast popped out and got the butter out of the fridge.

Nancy pinned the list of who'd sent Christmas cards to the bulletin board by the office, then sat down at the table again while Amy ate her toast. "So how does it feel to be back?" she asked.

"It's great," Amy said. "I mean, I love being at college, but there's nowhere like Heartland."

Nancy looked thoughtful. "That's true," she agreed. "But there are other special places, too. Sometimes it's good to remember that." She pushed her chair back. "Well, I'd better get started on lunch. Lou will be back in about an hour. Is that a good time for you, too?"

"Perfect. I'll be hungry again by then! I'll tell Ty," said Amy, finishing off her toast. "Thanks, Nancy. I don't know what we'd do without you!"

When Amy and Ty walked into the kitchen an hour later, it was full of the wonderful smell of spicy winter vegetable soup. Lou was sitting at the table feeding Holly spoonfuls of pureed carrot – most of which was ending up on Lou's clothes, as far as Amy could see – and Jack was washing his hands at the sink. It really felt like old times and Amy felt a rush of happiness.

As Nancy ladled out the soup, Jack asked how it had gone with the Breakspears.

"Well, they're very caring owners," said Amy, reaching for the basket of crusty brown bread.

"The problem seems to be tied in with Flamenco's breeding," said Ty. "Julia's very proud of her Andalusian bloodline – so on one hand, this is what Julia has chosen as her next horse–"

"–but on the other, she seems to expect Flamenco to be just like Logris, her old horse," Amy finished for him.

"Exactly," said Ty. "From what the Breakspears told me when they first brought Flamenco over, they've only had warmbloods before."

"Does that make a difference?" inquired Nancy.

"Totally," said Amy. "Warmblooded horses such as Hanoverians and Cleveland Bays, both good dressage breeds, tend to be much calmer and a lot more predictable than hot-blooded breeds such as Arabians and Thoroughbreds. Working with an Andalusian must have come as a bit of a shock for Julia."

"It's understandable that Julia sees all of Flamenco's unpredictable behaviour as negative," said Ty. "She doesn't know how to embrace it . . ."

". . . so she's trying to push Flamenco into being something she's not," concluded Amy. She scraped the bottom of her soup bowl. "No wonder Flamenco's getting so irritable." She looked across at Ty, and their eyes locked for a moment as they thought it through.

"She's probably confused," said Ty, speaking directly to Amy as though there was no one else in the room. "Southern European breeds like that have tons of initiative. They're all about stamina and speed and independence. You can't just put them in a box, real or metaphorical – they'll use all their will to break out of it."

There was a brief silence. Then Lou caught Amy's eye and grinned. "I'd never believe you've been away for five months," she said. "It's good to see you two still work so well together, no matter how much your lives change."

Amy swallowed. After all, she was the one whose life had changed, who had moved away . . . she was suddenly relieved that Ty had dealt with it so well.

She met Lou's gaze. "I can't believe it, either," she replied honestly. "I guess some things never change."

After lunch was over, Amy was anxious to put their thoughts into action right away. "How about we move Flamenco to the big paddock?" she suggested as Ty pulled his boots back on. "We could move the horses around so that she's in with calm companions. Then there'll be no chance for her to get hurt."

"Sounds good," agreed Ty. "She needs to stretch her legs a bit. How about putting her with just Libby and Bear? Neither of them will bother her."

At the moment, the horses were turned out as they'd been the day before – Libby and Bear in the smaller top paddock with Sundance, the others sharing the big field off the driveway. "We could leave Aria in the big paddock, too," Amy said. "She's really gentle. But we'll need to move all the others around."

Ty nodded. "Yeah, that sounds about right," he said. "Will you be OK to do all that yourself?"

"Oh!" Amy was surprised. "Well, I guess so. You're not free?"

Ty looked apologetic. "I've got the afternoon off," he said. "I said I'd help a friend out, moving some stuff in my pickup."

Amy could feel her face falling. Quickly, she tried to smile. "Of course, that's fine," she managed. "Sorry, I forgot you. . ."

"Don't live here?" Ty finished for her, jokingly. He grinned. "Don't worry, I'll be back tomorrow. Join-up with Flamenco followed by Spindle's second trail ride?"

Amy grinned back. "Sounds like a plan." She turned to Lou and Nancy. "Do you need some help cleaning up?"

"No, you head out," said Lou. "Holly will be taking her afternoon nap soon, so I'll have plenty of time. Nancy and Jack are going shopping."

"Yup, we thought Santa could use a hand," said Jack. "Didn't we, Nancy?"

Nancy gave Jack a quick smile. "Well, I hope we don't have to be *too* helpful," she said. "I've got my own lists to worry about."

"Oh, I think *I'll* be willing to let you out of my sight for half an hour or so," said Jack. "But I'm not so sure about *Santa.* He's very demanding."

"Yes, typical male," joked Nancy. "Never a moment's peace!"

Chapter Five

"You're not remotely sleepy, are you?" asked Lou, bouncing Holly up and down on her knee as Amy shrugged on her coat again. "All those people at lunch were just too exciting."

Holly was staring at Amy over Lou's shoulder, watching her aunt in fascination. The baby gurgled happily and stuck her fist in her mouth.

Lou wrapped her arms around her daughter and looked at Amy. "You know, I might bring her out to the yard for half an hour. You haven't formally met Nickel yet, have you?"

It took a few more minutes, but soon Holly was wrapped up in lots of warm clothes, and they headed out to the paddocks to catch the little chestnut Shetland.

"He's so easy to bring in," said Lou as the tiny pony trotted up to them. "The smallest chance of some horse cookies and he heads for the gate like an arrow!"

Amy bent down to slip a halter over the tiny pony's ears and watched in delight as her little niece reached out for Nickel's fluffy golden mane. Holly squealed in excitement when Lou lifted her on to his sturdy, furry back. With Lou holding Holly firmly in place, Amy led the Shetland forward. Holly's eyes were wide with delight as she dug her little hands into his thick winter coat.

"Something tells me we've got another rider in the family!" Amy laughed. "So come on, Lou, tell me: How long did it take you to find Sugarfoot's twin?"

Lou raised her eyebrows. "Oh, I didn't even have to look! Didn't I tell you? Scott found him and bought him to surprise me. I burst into tears when I saw him."

"I'm not surprised!" exclaimed Amy, knowing that Sugarfoot would always hold a special place in Lou's heart.

"Scott spotted him at a client's farm," Lou continued. "The farmer was saying they needed to find a good home for him because his daughter had moved on to a bigger pony. Scott knew I'd adore him. And he thought it would be good to get Holly started with a little pony that we know is safe. It was the biggest surprise."

"He cares about you so much," Amy said softly. She looked at her sister's happy face. They had been happy before – Scott was so caring, and Amy couldn't imagine a better match for Lou – but Holly seemed to have brought them even closer.

Lou nodded. "He sure does. Both of us," she added,

hugging Holly. She gazed around at the beautiful winter landscape. "When I was working in New York, I never imagined I'd end up living here. Now I don't think I could live anywhere else."

Amy smiled. "I guess you won't have to."

"No. Not unless Scott decides he wants to leave. And if he does, of course I'd go with him. I just want to be wherever he is, really."

It was so unlike Lou to sound so romantic that Amy was on the verge of teasing her, but then she saw that Lou's cheeks had gone pink and that she was avoiding looking at her sister.

"Well, I just hope he doesn't get a bad attack of the travel bug anytime soon," said Amy lightly.

She patted Nickel's soft neck. Would she ever feel that way about someone? she wondered. Before she started college, it was how she'd felt about Ty. But that hadn't stopped her from leaving, had it? She'd willingly thrown herself into her new life, her studies, and everything else that college had to offer. Well, *almost* everything. *I'm still single,* she reminded herself. But right now, it was hard to imagine being any other way.

Meanwhile, here she was, back at home. Living the life she loved, as though she'd never been away. Her mind drifted to what had happened over lunch: how Ty had flushed at Lou's comment. It was the only sign he'd given, aside from the awkwardness between them when she first arrived, of what might be going on underneath the surface. Had he really accepted their breakup. . . ? Amy clicked her tongue to keep the little Shetland moving and pushed the thought away.

Lou decided that one loop of the paddock was enough for Holly, especially since it was so cold. She lifted her off the Shetland's back and headed back to the farmhouse to put her down for her afternoon nap. Amy stayed outside to sort the horses into the paddocks. In another half hour, all the horses were in their new locations, and Amy went to the little paddock behind the barn to catch Flamenco.

The Andalusian had finished half of her hay, but she wasn't eating when Amy arrived. Instead, she was standing in one corner looking over the fence towards the top paddock where Sundance, Jasmine, Nickel, and Spindle were drifting apart from one another as they settled down to graze. The beautiful chestnut mare was whinnying to them, her ears pricked.

Amy called her name but wasn't surprised when she didn't respond. Flamenco wasn't interested in people right now. So Amy opened the gate and approached her slowly, a handful of horse cookies at the ready.

Flamenco saw her and wheeled around, then cantered off across the paddock. This made sense to Amy: If Flamenco wasn't given her freedom on a regular basis, she wouldn't be happy to give it up in a hurry. Catching her could take some time. She decided to get a bucket to rattle the treats in, but Flamenco still wasn't interested.

Next Amy tried cornering her, but that was hopeless, too – Flamenco was a powerful mare with lightning reflexes, and Amy didn't stand a chance.

At last, she had an inspiration. The thing that Flamenco seemed to crave almost as much as freedom was time in the open with other horses. She thought it through carefully, then brought Bear from the bottom paddock and turned him out with Flamenco. The mare greeted him with a trumpeting whinny and cavorted around him despite the fact that all Bear did was make a beeline for her leftover hay. Amy smiled and left them alone for a while.

Half an hour later, she returned to catch Bear again. As usual, the placid gelding was perfectly happy for her to lead him back to the gate. But Flamenco was furious. She whinnied in desperation as Bear plodded out of the paddock, and Amy knew her chance had come. She tied Bear up and approached Flamenco again, a halter hidden behind her back. The trick worked. The mare allowed her to slip the halter over her ears, then lipped up her reward of treats.

"Now you're going to get a real reward," Amy told her as she led the two horses down the track. "Lots of space and lots of company. You'll like that, won't you?"

Sure enough, Flamenco was delighted. As soon as Amy released her, she tore around the big paddock, bucking and twisting like a wild salmon. Bear and Libby looked on, amused, but Aria responded to the show; she cantered up to Flamenco with her tail held high, then the two horses set off at a gallop like a couple of yearlings.

Amy wished that Julia Breakspear could be there to see how gorgeous her mare looked when she was allowed to behave naturally. It was exhilarating to witness how full of joy Flamenco was, flicking her heels into the air and tossing her head; she clearly hadn't been able to do anything like this for . . . how long? And it showed Amy something else, too: Essentially, the mare was happy. Given the chance to show it, she loved life and she loved company. And a horse like that could always be reached on an emotional level, as long as her spirit wasn't challenged and constrained in the process. It was simply up to Amy and Ty to find the right way to communicate with Flamenco and channel her limitless energy.

With only half the afternoon left, Amy left the paddock and walked to the barn. Both Apollo and Red needed exercising, so she gave them each a good hour in the school, working them through their paces and over a small course of jumps. As the daylight began to fade, she saw Lou waving at the gate.

"I have to go!" she called. "I promised Scott I'd cook tonight. Is that OK?"

"Fine!" Amy called back. "See you tomorrow."

After Lou had gone, Amy finished up with Red and led him back up to the barn. She untacked him, gave him a quick rubdown, and settled him in for the night, then she went out to the paddocks to bring all the horses in. It felt strange when she realized that she was the only person left at Heartland at the moment. Usually, there would be a spare pair of hands to lead a couple of horses in, but Jack and Nancy still weren't back, and there was no one else. Not that it mattered. The air was bitterly cold, and the horses were all too glad to see her with her hands full of halters, knowing they would get fed in the nice warm barn. Even Flamenco had used up much of her energy and consented to being caught without a fuss.

By the time Amy finished the evening chores, it was totally dark and the wind had risen, filled with handfuls of icy hail. As she headed back to the farmhouse, huddled into her coat, she thought of the roads icing up and began to worry. She wished she'd asked what time Jack and Nancy thought they'd be back; she was sure Grandpa would have said if he wasn't going to be around for the evening.

Back in the kitchen, she fixed herself a sandwich and decided to try Jack's mobile phone. It was switched off, so she left a message and wandered into the living room, trying not to let her imagination get the best of her. *No news is good news,* she told herself: if anything had happened, it wouldn't take long for her to find out. She decided to light a fire and soon had a blaze going in the grate. She sat gazing at it, keeping one ear open for the sound of a car on the drive.

By nine p.m., there was still no sign of Jack and Nancy, and Amy began to think through her options. She could call Lou. She could call Nancy's house. She could call the police and check to be sure there hadn't been any accidents. In the end, she decided the most sensible option was to call Nancy. She found the number in the office phone book and dialled it, her heart beating slightly faster.

She heard the phone ringing, but after five rings she knew that no one was going to answer. She let it ring a while longer, then replaced the receiver. Now what?

Was it really worth worrying Lou? She and Scott wouldn't have any better idea of what had happened – in an emergency, all of Jack's ID would point to Heartland. And calling the police seemed a bit extreme; after all, Amy wasn't even sure what their plans had been. She would just have to wait.

Even with the fire spitting, it was chilly in the living room, so Amy got her comforter from her room and made herself a mug of hot chocolate. She snuggled into an armchair and tried to read a magazine, but the words danced in front of her and refused to sink in. At last, she dozed off uneasily, the magazine slipping from her fingers.

She woke with a jerk. There was a car in the driveway, at last! She threw off the comforter and ran through the kitchen to peer out of the front window.

"Thank goodness," she breathed. It was Grandpa's pickup.

As soon as Jack walked through the door, weighed down with shopping bags, Amy flung her arms around him. "Grandpa!" she exclaimed. "Where were you?"

Jack dumped the bags on the kitchen floor. He looked tired. "Honey, I'm sorry . . ." he began.

It was then that Amy realized he was alone. "Where's Nancy?" she demanded. "Didn't she come back with you?"

Jack shrugged off his heavy winter coat and hung it up. "No, she didn't," he said. "I took her home."

"But . . . I called her house," said Amy. "There was no answer. And I called your mobile – I almost called the police. . ."

Jack looked at her, regret showing in his eyes. "I took Nancy home after we finished in town. We had an . . . we had things to discuss, so we went for a pizza." He passed a hand over his face. "Sorry, Amy. My mobile's been off – the battery's dead. I should have let you know. . . ."

"It's OK, Grandpa." Amy studied his tired features, a pang of anxiety passing through her. What had Jack almost said? They'd had an . . . not *a,* but *an* . . . What? An *argument*? It wasn't like him to forget to call if he was going to be late. "Well . . . I mean, I hope everything's OK – it is, isn't it?"

"Yes, yes, everything's fine." Jack turned away and went to put the kettle on. As he lifted two mugs down from the cabinet, he glanced over his shoulder. "Nancy means a lot to you, doesn't she?"

Amy stared at his in surprise. "Yes, of course. She's like part of the family."

Jack took longer than usual to find a teaspoon. Amy felt her stomach flip over. What was he trying to say? That Nancy might not be part of the family any more?

"Grandpa, are you sure you're OK?"

"Yes, I'm sure. Now, how about having a hot drink with me? I'm frozen."

He didn't sound particularly OK, but it was clear the subject was closed.

Chapter Six

Amy lay in the dark, wondering what could have happened between Grandpa and Nancy. The thought of them splitting up was unbearable. She thought of his lively, happy face when he'd met her at the bus stop – and how different he'd looked tonight, worn out and weary. She thought of Nancy and Lou, and how much Holly loved Nancy already. It would just be too awful if things were going wrong. But why would they be? What could possibly be the problem?

The thoughts churned around her mind for a while, but it had been a long, physically exhausting day – more physical than most days at college – and in spite of herself, Amy fell asleep.

In the morning, Jack seemed his usual self; Amy came in from mucking out the stalls and found him whistling as he made himself coffee. She decided to push her worries aside. *Every couple has arguments,* she told herself. Jack and Nancy weren't any different just because they were older. When she heard Ty's pickup in the front yard, she headed out to meet him, determined to focus on the day ahead instead.

"How's our lively visitor doing?" Ty asked, slamming his pickup door.

"You should have seen her when I turned her out with the others yesterday!" Amy told him. "I don't think I've ever seen a horse so happy. She's a bit calmer this morning, though she wasn't too pleased when I led the other horses out and left her behind."

"It'll be interesting to see how she deals with join-up after a taste of freedom," said Ty. "Shall we give her a brush-down first?"

"Good idea," said Amy. "I'll get a grooming kit."

They headed down to the barn and found Flamenco banging her stall door in frustration.

"Hey, hey, steady, girl," Amy soothed her. "We'll have you outside soon."

With both of them giving her plenty of attention, the mare began to relax again, nibbling at Ty's jacket as he brushed her long, elegant legs.

"She needs stimulation, that's for sure," Amy commented. "She could make a fantastic dressage horse eventually, but it's going to take her a while."

"Yeah, probably," agreed Ty. "She needs to regain confidence in herself first. She'll want to experiment with feeling free for a lot longer than most horses. I wouldn't be surprised if join-up doesn't work right away."

Amy was surprised. She hadn't even considered the possibility that they might fail to join up with the Andalusian mare – but when she thought about it, she realized Ty might be right. The last thing Flamenco needed was more pressure, so all the ordinary schedules had to be thrown away. "Well, we can try," she said.

The grooming over, Amy led the mare out of the barn and down to the main school. Flamenco skittered and shied at everything, just as she had with Julia, but Amy ignored it. She was bound to be lively first thing in the morning, and Amy didn't want to draw too much attention to her bad behaviour. It would be better to concentrate on praising her when she did things well.

Ty watched from the gate as Amy led Flamenco to the middle of the school ring and unclipped the lead rein. The fiery horse stared at her for an instant, not quite believing she was free. Then, as she tossed her head up and down and realized it was true, she wheeled on her hindquarters and charged away full speed across the ring, straight for the railings.

Amy clapped hand to her mouth in horror, images of the mare smashing her legs running through her mind, or jumping the fence and careening off into the countryside.

"Ty! She's–"

"Don't worry! She's fine," Ty called out as Flamenco swerved away from the rails at the last moment.

Amy slowly let out her breath as the mare began galloping around the edge of the school ring instead. Maybe Julia was right – maybe she was just too wild to run loose like this. At that pace, it would be easy for her to injure herself, even if she didn't crash into or try to jump the fences. But it was too late now. They just had to allow her energy to take its course.

Gradually, to Amy's relief, Flamenco began to slow down. Her wild gallop became a canter and even showed signs of slowing to a trot. Whenever it did, Amy stepped towards her and drove her on again, not allowing the mare to rest. That was the key to join-up – making the horse realize that she didn't like being driven away; that what she really wanted was to be with the person in the centre of the ring.

But however many times she sent the mare off around the ring, Flamenco showed no signs of wanting to stop. On the contrary, she seemed determined to maintain her independence, cantering around and gathering speed whenever Amy got close. Sure, she was getting tired – her coat was dark with sweat, and her breathing was growing noisy. But that wasn't the same as acknowledging that Amy was part of her herd. She wasn't joining up.

After a while – much longer than it usually took for a horse to join up – Amy shrugged her shoulders. "I think you're right," she called to Ty. "She's not going to do it today. I'm worried about overworking her."

"I think that's OK," Ty said. "She's been cooped up for so long, she's bound to have some extra energy to burn off. She needs to relearn that she can be free and listen to her instincts, because she'll only be able to trust us when she trusts herself. She'll join up when she's ready."

It was disappointing, but it made sense. So far, human beings hadn't convinced Flamenco that they could be part of what she wanted for herself. Amy walked over to the gate and watched the mare, wondering what she would do when she was no longer being driven around the ring. If she wanted to be with Amy, she'd follow her to the gate – but it was soon clear that there was no chance of that happening today. Instead, Flamenco trotted to the far end of the ring with her tail held high. Then she turned around and stopped, regarding them with interest, but keeping her distance.

Ty grinned, shaking his head. "Look at her. She's fabulous, and she knows it."

"She sure does," said Amy. "But now we have to catch her."

It was easier to catch Flamenco than Amy expected. Ty rattled some horse cookies in a bucket and the mare reluctantly made her way towards him. She was clearly trying to figure out if there was some way she could get her head in the bucket without being caught. But the moment she lowered her head, Ty snapped the lead rope on to her halter.

They led her back up to the barn and, after giving her a thorough wipe-down to dry her off, they put her warm New Zealand rug back on. After just half an hour in the barn, Flamenco was already getting restless again.

Amy reached for the final buckle and peered over the mare's back at Ty. "Now for another rodeo when we turn her out," she said. "Hope you're ready for the show."

Ty clapped his hand on Flamenco's neck. "Wouldn't miss it for the world."

They led her down to the bottom paddock and she whinnied in excitement to her friends, particularly Aria, who looked up from grazing with her ears pricked. The mare flung her head around as Amy tried to unclip the lead rope, too distracted to pay attention. At last, Flamenco was free, and Amy waited for the spectacle.

But it didn't come. Flamenco cantered off towards Aria, but slowed to a floating trot with her tail kinked over her back. She stopped and touched noses with the gentle black mare, then gave her mane a shake and began to graze.

"Oh," said Amy. "So she's had enough of being wild for one day!"

"Don't sound so disappointed." Ty laughed. "As far as I can see, that's exactly what we wanted to achieve! Now that she's allowed to let off steam, she doesn't feel like she has to fight to express herself every opportunity she gets."

"Yes, I get that," Amy agreed. "I just hope she doesn't become *too* tame."

"I don't think there's much danger of that," said Ty.

He nudged her arm affectionately, and they leaned on the gate together, watching the mare in companionable silence.

The rest of the morning passed quickly. Amy rode Apollo again, this time around a larger course of jumps, and Ty gave Libby some schooling. After lunch, Amy got Spindle from the top paddock while Ty tacked up Red for their trail ride. Spindle stood quietly as Amy took off his rug and tacked him up, but when she swung herself into the saddle and directed him towards the trails, his ears pricked in excitement and he began to prance on the pavement of the front yard.

"I think it'd be good to let him stretch out a bit today," said Amy as Ty rode up alongside.

"Let's go the long way around the ridge then. We can canter to the top."

Amy nodded. She was excited. It was a beautiful route through the woods, and the long canter was always thrilling. She stroked Spindle's neck and nudged him forward with a squeeze of her calves.

They set out in single file, with Ty riding Red in front. Amy relaxed for the first mile or so, happy to walk and trot, enjoying the company of her young, eager horse. Once again, it seemed incredible that she'd been home for only a couple of days. She thought back to the first awkward hours in Ty's company. She'd been so nervous! But why? It didn't make any sense; after all, they'd been friends before they started dating, so why couldn't they be friends again? And already she felt so close to him again – closer than she was to anyone at college. The image of Will flitted through her mind and Amy smiled. He was a great guy, but somehow it just hadn't been right. She felt so lucky that Ty had been able to show her how good a relationship could be, and knew that she could never settle for something that felt less than perfect.

Ty twisted in his saddle and looked back with a smile. "Ready for a canter?"

Amy grinned at him. "You bet!"

Spindle was a fast learner and he already knew what "canter" meant. Amy had to restrain him for a second, to teach him that he could only go when she told him to and not before. Then, as he obediently checked his stride, she released the reins and pushed him on. They were soon at the top of the small hill in the woods, and she halted him, patting his neck enthusiastically.

"Don't worry, there'll be another one soon," she told him as he snorted and tossed his head.

They trotted along a winding trail through the woods, the horses' breath forming clouds in the cold air. A pheasant flew out from the undergrowth, and Spindle leaped sideways, almost knocking Amy out of the saddle. But he quickly regained his composure and trotted on without any more fuss. Amy was pleased. He was behaving with a lot of maturity for such a young horse; it was astonishing to think that he was a full three years younger than Flamenco. Maybe, she mused, there was something to be learned from that. Spindle had been allowed to develop naturally. She'd never pressured him or pushed his training in a particular direction. Instead, she'd worked with his instincts and built on the trust he'd naturally placed in her. As a result, he seemed to be progressing strongly and confidently.

They reached the slope that took them to the top of the ridge, and then set off at a canter once again. This time, Amy urged Spindle on, giving him the freedom to stretch out. It was exhilarating, and she laughed out loud as his long strides began to eat up the ground, chasing after Red's powerful hindquarters. By the time they reached the top, both horses were tiring and blowing hard, but were no less eager to keep going. Reluctantly, Amy reined Spindle in. The trail was beginning to narrow and it wasn't safe to keep going at that speed.

"That was fantastic!" Amy exclaimed as she drew up alongside Red. "He's so fast, but his canter's amazingly smooth."

Ty leaned forward and stroked Red's neck. "Bit different from Sundance, I should think," he said. "Spindle's a good hand taller."

Amy nodded. "Yes, Spindle's perfect for me," she said. She sighed and looked out over the view that stretched out before them – the woodland giving way to checkered farmland, with mountains way off in the distance. It was going to be hard to leave all this behind again when she went back to college.

They turned on to the trail that led back to Heartland, leaving the view behind to ride side by side through the forest. The horses' hoofbeats were muffled by the covering of pine needles on the ground, only striking loud and clear when their shoes knocked against a stone. They rounded a corner, and a gap opened up; a swath of trees had been felled by the foresters and Amy could see straight down on the fields below.

"You can see that mare from here," she said, pointing. "The pregnant one with the donkey friend."

They reined in the horses for a moment. The donkey was nosing a loose pile of hay in the corner of the field, but the dapple grey mare was standing with a hind leg resting, her belly looking enormous.

"Want to cut down that way? I'd like to take a closer look at her," Amy said.

"Sure," said Ty. "There's a new forestry trail coming up. That'll be the quickest way down."

"Seems like there's a lot of logging going on," commented Amy as they turned on to the trail. "Is it because of the lumberyard?"

"Yeah. They're making sure there's plenty of new

planting as well, though," said Ty. "A tree for a tree, that kind of thing. I've spoken to Mr. Middleton quite a lot about it. He grew up around here and he says he wants to keep the beauty of Clairdale Ridge intact even though he's in the lumber business. Future generations, that's his motto."

"He sounds like a good guy," Amy said.

"He is," said Ty.

They came out of the woods and trotted along the trail at the edge of the trees until they reached the mare's field. Spindle whinnied a greeting and the mare looked up, while the donkey snorted and began to walk over. Amy studied the mare, taking in her distended belly and the line of her tail. There was nothing obviously wrong with the pregnancy, but she felt uneasy.

"Ty, I'd like to examine her," she said. "Could you hold Spindle?" She dismounted and handed Ty the reins. "I won't be long."

She vaulted over the post-and-rail fence and walked slowly towards the mare, taking care not to startle her. The mare shifted her weight, but didn't try to move away. Amy gently stroked her neck and ran her hand along her back, then down towards her belly. The mare stamped a foot and looked around restlessly.

"It's OK, girl," Amy murmured. "I'm not going to hurt you."

After looking at her udder and the muscles around and under the mare's tail, she straightened up, frowning. Overall, the horse was in good health, there was no doubt about that, and Amy was glad to note that there was a shelter in one corner of the field to provide protection from the wind – but it wasn't the best birthing stall in the world. She walked back to the fence and jumped over it.

"What is it?" asked Ty. "D'you think she's got a problem?"

Amy shook her head. "Not a *problem,*" she said. "But she's closer to giving birth than I'd thought. She's slightly uneasy, and the muscles around her tail have relaxed. Her udder's beginning to fill, too."

Ty raised an eyebrow. "So how far off is she?"

"It's hard to be sure. Could be a couple of weeks, could be much less. She could have a New Year's baby – that's only nine days away." Amy swung herself back into Spindle's saddle. "I hope someone's monitoring her."

"I'm sure they are," Ty said. "But if the worst happened and she foaled unexpectedly, she could handle it on her own, right?"

"Well, it's true that animals are designed to give birth

and get right back on their feet," said Amy. "But they still need to be warm and comfortable. If the weather gets any worse, that little shed isn't really adequate for a new foal."

Ty looked thoughtful. "There's fresh hay in the field," he said. "I guess that means that someone must be visiting them regularly."

"Good point," Amy agreed. "I'm just surprised she's still outside full-time, that's all. I'd have taken her into a barn by now. It won't be easy to move her later. I think we should find out who the owners are and check in with them. Any ideas?"

"The Middletons own the field," said Ty. He hesitated. "I could find out from . . . from them."

"I think we should," said Amy. "I'd like to know that she's in good hands."

When they got back to the yard, it seemed to Amy more than ever that she and Ty were clicking in the comfortable way that they'd always shared: dividing up the evening chores, teasing each other as they brought in the horses, consulting about what to work on the next day. They had always been such a great team, Amy mused as she adjusted Flamenco's rugs for the night.

But there was more, too. An image of Ty's straight back riding ahead of her on Red that afternoon flashed through her mind; then the expression in his green eyes as he'd looked at her while they were discussing the pregnant mare. *Don't be stupid,* she scolded herself. They'd split up for really good reasons – because . . . well, because. . .

"Amy." Ty's voice broke into her thoughts, and she jumped guiltily.

"I'm almost done here–" she began.

"I'm pretty much finished, too. I'll be heading out soon." Ty leaned against the door post of Flamenco's stall, fiddling with his mobile phone. "I found out who owns the pregnant mare and donkey. It's a couple, Mr. and Mrs. Hayes. I jotted down the number for you." He handed her a scrap of paper. "Just thought it might be best if you call them, given your foaling knowledge."

"Sure." Amy pocketed the piece of paper. "Thanks. I'll call them in the morning."

"OK." Ty shoved his phone into his shirt pocket. "What are you up to later? Are you going out?"

Amy reached under Flamenco's belly for the last rug strap. "I hadn't planned on it."

"Still recovering from the end of term?"

"Something like that." Amy straightened up. "Soraya

and Matt aren't back yet, anyway. I'm not sure who else is around."

"Well, if you're free. . ." Ty seemed a little nervous, and cleared his throat. "I was wondering – I'm going to a Christmas party tonight, and I don't know . . . I just thought maybe you'd want to come?"

"Oh!" Amy's heart gave a leap, and she turned away, pretending to fiddle with the rug so that she could hide her face. When she looked up again, her expression was perfectly composed. "Well . . . I stayed home last night. It'd be good to go out for a change. Thanks, Ty."

"Good." Ty still seemed awkward, and he hesitated. "Right. Uh . . ." he began, then trailed off. "Well, I'll head home and change, then come back and pick you up. Is that OK?"

"Sure, that's great."

Their eyes met for a second, but Ty's slid away quickly. He frowned and seemed to be thinking about something.

Amy found that her mouth was dry. "Is . . . I mean. . ."

Ty turned back to her. "That's great," he said more decisively. "I can be here at about eight-thirty. Does that give you enough time?"

"Time for what?"

"Oh, you know . . . girl stuff," he said, grinning

lopsidedly.

"Don't worry. I'll be ready," said Amy, laughing. "See you at eight-thirty."

Ty gave a little wave and headed out of the barn. Amy patted Flamenco, trying to push down a feeling of nervous anticipation inside her. Why on earth was she so excited? Ty's friends were nice, but Amy had just come back from a solid two weeks of partying at college. This would probably be nothing compared to some of the events she'd been to recently.

But as she walked up to the front yard, Amy found herself breaking into a smile. The truth was, it didn't matter what the party was like. Even if there were only three people there, she knew she'd enjoy it – she and Ty always had a good time, wherever they were. And tonight would be no exception, she was sure.

Chapter Seven

Amy popped into the feed room to turn out the lights, then hurried back into the farmhouse. To her surprise, Jack was there on his own, cooking some sausages on the stove.

"Hey, honey, you hungry?" he asked her as she pulled off her boots. "I'm going to have these on a roll with some salad. I'm cooking enough for you."

"Sure," said Amy. "Thanks, Grandpa." She hesitated. "Isn't Nancy coming over?"

Jack shook his head. "No, no. She's busy. Got lots to do with Christmas coming up." He was turning the sausages and didn't look at her.

Amy wanted to ask more, but something in Jack's voice warned her not to. "Have I got time to change first? Ty's asked me to go to a party with him."

"Sure, you go ahead. Glad to hear you're heading out – you've done nothing but work from the minute you got back."

He sounded cheerful enough, and Amy pushed her worries to the back of her mind. "Thanks, Grandpa. See you in a minute."

She bounded up the stairs, stripped off her work clothes, and dived into the shower. Having met Ty's friends once before, she knew it wouldn't be a dressy party. Back at Easter when she'd been home, she and Ty had met up with his friends and she'd gotten all dressed up – then felt dumb when she realized she was the only one who was spiffed up. She didn't want to make the same mistake again.

So, with a towel wrapped around her head, Amy rummaged for her favourite jeans, faded ones that fit like old friends. She pulled them on, then hunted for a shirt. She found a couple of strappy tops and looked at them longingly for a second. She resisted the temptation, and found a plain blue button-down shirt instead. Aquamarine blue . . . the same blue as the dress she'd worn that night before she left for college, when Ty had pulled out an Irish friendship ring to slip on to her finger. . . *Stop it,* she told herself. *It's just a shirt.*

She put it on. Ty wouldn't make the connection; guys didn't think of things like that. She dragged a comb through her hair and decided to leave it down, applied a subtle line of eyeliner and put aside a lip gloss to apply after dinner. She was done.

Downstairs, Jack was sitting in the living room with a tray on his lap. "Hope you don't mind me abandoning the kitchen," he said. "I put the sausages in the oven to keep them warm for you. There's a show coming up about fly-fishing, and I just thought, since you're heading out. . ."

"That's totally fine, Grandpa. Thanks!" Amy helped herself to some food and sat with him to eat it.

After the meal was finished, she took their trays into the kitchen and ran back upstairs to brush her teeth and apply her lip gloss. She looked at herself critically in the mirror. *Laid back,* the reflection told her. No one would be able to accuse her of trying too hard – not this time! She glanced down at the Claddagh ring on her finger, remembering what Ty had told her that night: *If your heart is free, you wear the heart facing outward. But if your heart belongs to someone, you wear it facing in.* When they'd split up, she'd turned the ring around so that the heart faced outward. She toyed with it for a second, wondering if Ty had noticed the statement she was making with the ring – and if he had, what he felt about it.

She heard the sound of a car coming up the driveway and ran downstairs to say good night to Jack. He was looking thoughtful when she returned to the living room. Even though he was watching the TV Amy found it hard to believe he was this interested in fly-fishing. The nagging sense that things weren't quite right returned, and Amy felt a pang of anxiety about leaving him on his own.

"Are you sure you don't mind me going out, Grandpa?" she asked.

Jack waved his hand at her. "Don't you worry," he told her. "Of course I don't mind. You go out and enjoy yourself." Ty's car horn honked outside, and Jack reached for the TV remote and began flipping channels.

Amy hesitated. "OK, if you're sure," she said. "I'll see you later."

"I doubt it," Jack teased. "I suspect I'll be tucked in bed by the time you get back. See you for breakfast in the morning!"

Amy laughed, and bent down to kiss his cheek. "OK, Grandpa. Have a nice evening."

A blast of icy air hit her as she ran out to Ty's pickup. He leaned across and opened the door for her and she scrambled in, putting her coat tight around her.

"You look nice," he told her.

"Oh, thanks," said Amy, trying not to sound too pleased. Why had he said that? He couldn't really see how she looked in the dark with her coat on. Perhaps it was just habit; he'd always been good at giving compliments. But could it be that he'd wanted to express something more?

They had always been on the same wavelength, which meant Ty must have noticed how quickly they had gotten close again. It was like she hadn't been away at college at all. . .

The pickup bounced down the driveway, and Ty took a left at the road.

"We're not going into town?" Amy asked.

Ty shook his head. "Didn't I say? The party's at the lumberyard."

"The one on Clairdale Ridge?"

"Yup. They invited half the town as near as I can tell. That's OK with you, isn't it?" Ty sounded apologetic, almost flustered.

"Of course it is," Amy reassured him.

All the same, she was a little surprised. She'd imagined a smaller gathering in someone's house or maybe in one of the restaurants in town. The Middletons had wasted no time getting established, she mused; throwing a big Christmas party was pretty ambitious. But that was a good thing. It was nice to know that there were friendly, outgoing people near Heartland – after all, anyone living on the ridge was pretty much a neighbour.

They followed a winding back road that climbed part of the way up the ridge and then wound back on itself through the forest. The lumberyard looked like a completely different place compared to how it appeared from their trail ride in the daylight. The yard and driveway were packed with cars and the buildings were covered with twinkling lights. Music filled the air – it sounded like a live band playing – and, as Amy stepped out of the pickup, she heard the buzz of lots of voices.

Around the corner of the yard, one of the big barns was filled with people. Sure enough, there was a band playing catchy rock songs on a makeshift stage in one corner, and in the open barn door there was a row of big outdoor heaters. An enormous Christmas tree stood just outside, lit from top to bottom with sparkling silver lights.

Ty led Amy inside, nodding and smiling to people as they passed. Amy saw curiosity flicker in some of the faces as their glances shifted from Ty's face to hers. She didn't recognize any of them, even though she looked for the people she'd met during spring break.

Ty touched her elbow. "It's pretty busy by the food table. If you hang out here a minute, I'll go get us something to drink." He plunged into the thickest part of the crowd, leaving Amy to look at the scene around her. It seemed like there was a big mix of people – mostly in their late teens and twenties, but quite a few older faces, too. In front of the band some of the girls were beginning to dance.

A girl close to Amy caught her eye, and smiled. "Did you come with Ty?" she asked.

Amy smiled back. "Yes – are you friends with him?"

The girl nodded. "Yeah, we see him around a lot. I'm Sandy and this is Josh." She indicated the blond guy standing next to her.

"I guess you know about Heartland, then," Amy said, fishing for clues. "I'm Amy Fleming. I'm back on holiday from college."

Josh looked vague. "Heartland?"

"You know, Josh, it's that horse hospital place over the ridge," said Sandy. "The place where Ty works."

Amy balked at Heartland being described as a horse hospital, but she kept her smile fixed in place. "That's right," she said. "It's great working with Ty again. College is fun, but it's not the same as working with horses the whole time. I really miss not riding every day."

Sandy laughed. "I don't know how you do it," she said. "I'm scared stiff of horses. I think it's the teeth – all yellow and scary, like tombstones."

Amy thought of Flamenco's wild beauty as she cantered around the paddock and tried to think of something to say.

"You don't ride, then," she said. She knew it sounded dumb, and she wished Ty would hurry up with those drinks.

Sandy shook her head. "Not on your life. I stick to safer things – like fast cars." She laughed. "But Ty's pretty crazy about horses, isn't he?"

"He has to be," put in Josh.

"Well, yes, he loves them," said Amy. "Everyone at Heartland does." She smiled again, and decided it was time to escape. "I think I'd better go see what he's up to."

Sandy and Josh nodded, perfectly at ease. "Nice to meet you, Amy. See you later."

Amy made her way across the barn to the back, where there was a long table serving root beer and mulled cider at one end and plates of ribs and chicken wings at the other. Ty didn't seem to be among the people milling around there, so she peered over the sea of heads, looking for his familiar figure. At last, she spotted him holding two glasses of root beer, almost hidden from view by the two guys he was chatting with near the dance floor. She made her way over.

"Amy!" Ty spotted her as she approached. "I was just coming to find you." He handed her one of the glasses and indicated the two guys. "Come and say hello to Jed

Middleton – his dad owns the lumberyard. And this is Chesman. Chesman Davies."

"Nice to meet you." Amy shook hands with both of them, and noticed that they had rough, workmen's palms and weatherbeaten faces. Chesman grinned at her and looked her in the eye a little too directly. Hastily, she switched her gaze to Jed instead.

"I guess you've met my sister," said Jed.

Amy was confused. "I don't think so," she said. "Should I have?"

"He means Heather," Ty explained.

Amy realized he was talking about the girl who had been riding Sundance the day she arrived. "Oh," she said. She hadn't realized that Heather was a Middleton. "Well, I've seen her, but we haven't met. I hear she's been a lot of help at Heartland."

Jed seemed a little surprised and looked questioningly at Ty. Then he grinned. "Yeah, you could say that."

From their exchange of glances, Amy guessed that Ty knew Jed pretty well. It made her feel slightly awkward, as though one year away from home had made her a stranger in town. She wished that Ty would come and stand a bit closer to her, but another of his friends tapped him on the shoulder and he turned away to chat.

Aware that Chesman was still eyeing her, Amy decided to direct her comments to Jed. "So, you work here with your dad?"

"Yup."

Jed started scanning the room as if he was looking for someone, and didn't seem to have much more to say. Amy swigged her root beer to cover the moment. It was Chesman who broke the silence. "You're at vet college, aren't you?" he asked, sounding curious.

"Yes. I'm in my second year now. Did Ty tell you?" Amy glanced over to see if Ty had finished talking, but his back was still turned.

Chesman had pale blue eyes that seemed all the paler against his deeply tanned skin. "Bet they work you hard there, don't they?"

Amy dodged his gaze, looking at a spot just over his right shoulder. "Well, yes. But I love the practical work, so it's never boring."

"I have a cousin who works in a vet's office," Chesman told her. "He works long hours, which seems pretty dull to me."

"Just getting a snack, Ches," Jed butted in. "You want something?"

Chesman nodded as Jed headed for the table. Now that

Amy was on her own with him, he touched her arm and jerked his head in the direction of the dance floor. "You wanna dance?"

Amy looked around again for Ty. If she was going to dance with anyone, she wanted it to be him, and she didn't want to give the impression she was heading off with someone else. But just at that moment, he turned towards her, as though he'd overheard Chesman's offer. "Go on, Amy," he said, his eyes warm and encouraging. "It'll be fun. Just make sure you save a dance for me later."

Amy flashed him a smile. "OK, it's a deal."

With that, she allowed Chesman to lead her on to the dance floor. It was getting crowded now, and they were jostled closer together by the other dancers, but it was an upbeat song, so Chesman couldn't hold her too close. Instead, he started in enthusiastically, shaking his shoulders and doing a bad Elvis impression. Amy laughed, trying to relax.

"You're a great dancer!" Chesman called to her above the music.

Amy shook her head. "Not to this, I'm not."

Chesman moved in closer. "So what's your scene, then?" he asked, putting his mouth close to her ear.

Uh-oh, thought Amy. Subtle this guy was not.

"It depends," she said, backing off and accidentally stepping on someone's toes. She spun around apologetically. "Sorry!"

The song was coming to an end and when she turned back to Chesman, she found he was studying her closely. "I'd like to find out," he said in a husky voice as they walked off the dance floor. "How'd you like to hang out after New Year's?"

Amy stared at him. He was probably a decent enough guy, she could see that. He was just . . . well, all sorts of things, and none of them was what she wanted. Not *remotely* what she wanted. She didn't want to hurt his feelings, but somehow she had to get the message across – loud and clear. In a flash of inspiration, she touched her claddagh ring and glanced at Ty on the other side of the barn.

"That's nice of you, Chesman," she said. "I'm sorry, it's just that . . . well, I'm not exactly free to say yes."

Chesman followed her glance, from the ring to Ty and back again. He frowned. "You mean. . . ?" he began, looking puzzled. "But–"

"Thanks for the dance though," Amy cut in. She didn't wait for him to finish – after all, she didn't want to *lie* to him, exactly – but it would be a whole lot easier if he came to his own conclusions. She smiled at him. "You don't know where the bathroom is, do you?"

"Sure," said Chesman, still looking bewildered. "There's one around the corner, outside the barn."

"Thanks. I'll see you later." Amy slipped away and headed out of the barn. She didn't really need the bathroom, but it was good to feel the fresh night air. She breathed in deeply, smoothing her hair back behind her ears. She felt bad about Chesman, but it was only a white lie – one she hadn't even spelled out. *And maybe it won't be a lie by the end of the evening,* whispered a voice in her head. The way she and Ty had gotten so close again couldn't just be part of their professional relationship, could it? Their connection had survived Amy being away for more than a year – that had to mean something. She twisted the ring around her finger, then, feeling composed again, she pushed back through the crowd.

She made her way around the dance floor, looking around to check out what had happened to Chesman. She spotted him standing with a big group of guys near the table gulping down a glass of root beer. He had his back turned to her. Amy sighed with relief and made her way to where she'd last seen Ty.

Ty was still chatting to the same friend, but he'd been joined by someone else, too. Amy saw that it was Heather

Middleton. She ran through all the details she knew about her in her mind. It would be good to meet her; they could swap notes about riding Sundance and laugh about what a character he was. Feeling more confident, she stepped forward, a smile ready on her lips.

After taking two steps closer, her smile froze. She stopped. Ty's arm . . . it couldn't be. She stared.

It was. Ty's arm was around Heather's waist. Heather was leaning into him, laughing at something. Ty was shaking his head and laughing, too, then he looked down into Heather's eyes. Heather reached up with her hand and touched Ty's face. As Amy watched, her heart plummeting, the petite blonde girl she'd seen riding *her* pony stood on tiptoe and pressed her lips to Ty's.

Chapter Eight

Quickly, before they could see her, Amy turned away. Why, why, why hadn't Ty told her he was with someone? Chesman's face swam in front of her eyes – his frown, the bewilderment. . . Amy felt her cheeks flush scarlet. She'd practically told him that she and Ty were dating. No wonder he had looked puzzled!

She began to make her way out of the barn, but it was too late. A surge of people just arriving pushed her back around the side of the table and before she knew it, she was standing opposite Ty.

Their eyes met. Amy's knew that her own were flashing, but she hoped her hurt didn't show. Ty's eyes were anxious, embarrassed – but somehow eager, too.

"Amy!" He was suddenly by her side. "Come and meet Heather. She's dying to say hello."

Is she really? Amy thought, struggling to keep control. She glanced up at Ty, trying to put as much meaning into that look as she could muster. *Isn't there something you forgot to mention?* she wanted to shout.

But Ty's gaze was already turned away from her, searching for Heather. The blonde girl came up to them, smiling, and offered her hand for Amy to shake. Feeling dazed, Amy shook it, taking in the pretty face, the perfect-looking blonde hair, the designer jeans, and the delicate strappy top embroidered with tiny beads and sequins. Suddenly, she felt underdressed and plain.

She realized that Heather was talking to her. "I've heard so much about you," she was saying. "And Sundance is so much fun! I just love riding him and it's taught me so much. Of course, Ty's taught me more than anything," she finished, smiling up at him, her blue eyes full of adoration.

"I–" Amy's voice came out as a squeak, and she cleared her throat. "I'm glad you like him," she managed to say. "Sundance, I mean." She felt as though her face was made of cardboard, her smile fixed in place with glue.

Heather nodded, her face alight. "He's just great," she enthused. "We even did some jumping over the logs up on the ridge last week. He threw in a couple of bucks and I almost fell off. Didn't I, Ty?"

Ty grinned. "All in a day's work to Sundance!" he said. "You're doing really well, though – it was like you became a totally different rider over the summer."

Heather's eyes sparkled with pleasure. "Thanks to you," she replied.

Amy felt sick.

The band started a new track, a classic Christmas love song, and Heather put her hand on Ty's arm. "I *love* this," she said. "Come on, let's dance. You don't mind, do you, Amy?"

Amy shook her head helplessly and watched as Heather led Ty away to join the other couples who were taking to the dance floor. Questions raged through her mind: How long had they been together? Heather had been riding Sundance *over the summer* – so they'd probably been together for months! *Why* hadn't Ty told her? Was he trying to protect her feelings, as if she wouldn't be able to cope with him dating someone else? She felt like a complete idiot. She went to the table and grabbed a fresh root beer, then wove her way back across the barn and out into the yard.

It was fine for Ty to be seeing Heather. Of course it was. It was just that he'd kept it a secret. It had never occurred to her that all the time she was talking to him about what was happening at Heartland, he had been teaching his new girlfriend how to ride on Amy's *own pony.*

No, that wasn't fair. Amy took a sip of the root beer. Chesman and Jed would think she was pretty weird, that was for sure. She thought of what she'd said about Heather being "a lot of help" at Heartland. No wonder Jed had grinned. Amy winced, feeling her cheeks grow hot all over again in spite of the biting winter air. She wished she could just leave and head home, but there was no way of getting there – not without asking Ty for a ride. And she definitely wasn't going to do *that*.

"Hey!" A voice interrupted her thoughts. A guy in a red-checked shirt was waving a hand in front of her face. "Anyone home?"

Amy smiled awkwardly.

"It's way too cold out here," said the guy. "You'll freeze. Come on, I'll take you in for a dance."

"It's OK, really," Amy protested. She searched for something to say. "Thanks, but I'm . . . I'm kind of waiting for someone. For a phone call."

The guy looked at her doubtfully. "Oh. Well, OK," he said. "You sure you're OK?"

Amy nodded. The kindness in his voice got to her, and she felt tears pricking at the back of her throat. But she managed to swallow them back. "Really. I'm fine. Thanks." She fished her mobile out of her bag and played with it, willing the guy to move away.

By some miracle, the phone began to ring. Amy was so surprised she almost dropped it, but then she saw the name on the screen and her heart leaped with relief. It was Soraya.

"Soraya! Am I glad to hear from you!"

"Amy! I just got home last night. I'm dying to see you. I've got sooo much to tell you. I can't believe it, Anthony's actually coming for Christmas Day – Christmas *Day* – because his folks are on holiday in New Mexico and he didn't want to go with them. I only have three days to get ready for him."

Anthony was Soraya's boyfriend. She'd split up with their old friend Matt soon after going to drama college, and Anthony had come on the scene a couple of months later. He was tall, wore trendy, dark-rimmed glasses, and played the trombone. "Fantastic," Amy said, hoping her voice didn't sound too flat. She had met Anthony briefly during her spring break last year and he'd seemed great, but the thought of seeing someone right now that she didn't know well made her even more anxious.

"So I have to catch up on all the gossip before he comes," Soraya carried on. "Where are you? Are you at Heartland? I don't think I can wait a whole day to see you. Can I come over?"

In spite of herself, Amy laughed. "No, I'm at a party."

"A party! I was wondering what all that noise was!

What kind of a party? Should I come there?"

Amy's laughter faded away. "Sure, you could. It's pretty crazy. But to be honest, I'd rather leave." Her voice cracked a little. "Soraya, is there any way you could come pick me up?"

There was a brief silence, and Amy knew that her friend had recognized the strain in her voice. "Sure I will," said Soraya. "Where are you?"

Amy gave her directions to the lumberyard. "I'll be waiting outside," she said. "By the Christmas tree."

"I'm on my way. You hang in there." Soraya's voice was brisk.

Amy flipped her phone shut and put it back in her bag. She walked back into the crowd and put her glass down on one of the tables, then braced herself. She was going to have to speak to Ty.

He was still on the dance floor, but the song was coming to an end. He and Heather separated, smiling, and walked back towards the main table. To Amy's relief, one of Heather's girlfriends took her to one side and started chatting with her, leaving Ty to make his way across the barn alone.

Amy reached his side and touched his arm. "Ty."

He looked around. "Oh, hi, Amy. I hope you didn't mind

us going off like that. . ."

"No, that's fine. Actually I just came to tell you I'm leaving."

"Leaving?" Ty's eyebrows shot up. "Why? Is everything OK? It's not because of. . . ?" He trailed off, running a hand through his hair.

Amy looked him directly in the eye. "No. It's not because of Heather." She paused. "You should have told me, though."

"I know." Ty looked at his feet. "I'm sorry, Amy. I know I should have . . . I just didn't know how." His eyes met hers again. "It is OK, isn't it? Look, we can talk about it–"

"It's fine." Amy gave a little shrug. "Let's not talk about it now. Soraya's on her way and we're going to catch up."

Ty's face cleared with relief. "Is she coming here?"

"Yeah, she's picking me up. Thanks for bringing me, Ty. I'll see you in the morning."

"OK. Thanks, Amy . . . I'll see–"

Amy didn't wait for the end of his sentence. She turned her back on him and started making her way back to the door. Just then, Ty Baldwin didn't have anything to say that she wanted to hear.

Amy was stamping her feet to stay warm when Soraya's sporty red car pulled into the yard, its lights blazing. She ran towards it and pulled open the passenger door.

"Soraya!" She leaned across and gave her friend a hug.

They held each other tight for a second, then pulled back to survey each other's faces.

"It's weird – every holiday I expect you to look different, and you don't," said Amy. "You look exactly the same, just a little more glamorous."

Soraya laughed, tossing her black curls over her shoulder. "I know exactly what you mean," she said. She reached down and turned up the car's heat. "Let's get you warmed up, then you can explain why you've been standing out in the cold instead of talking to all the cute guys at that party."

As Soraya turned the car around and roared off down the dark road that led to Heartland, Amy began her story. She told all about how awkward it had been with Ty when she first got back, how they'd quickly become close again as they'd started to work with Flamenco, and how she'd started to wonder whether there was still a spark between them. And then the party, about how she'd made a fool of herself with Jed and Chesman before the ultimate humiliation of seeing Heather kissing Ty.

"So, let's get this straight," said Soraya. "Ty's been seeing Heather for six months–"

"I don't know *exactly* how long," Amy admitted. "I have a feeling they got together over the summer."

"Over the summer," Soraya echoed. "It's December, Amy! And he didn't get around to telling you yet?"

"Not a single word," said Amy. "Not even the slightest hint."

"I can't believe it," said Soraya. "I seriously cannot believe it. That is so inexcusable."

"I know," Amy agreed. A dull thump of misery socked her in the stomach. "I just don't get it."

"And you didn't even guess when you got back?"

A fresh wave of embarrassment washed over Amy when she thought about how she'd read the situation. "No. Exactly the opposite. I thought . . . Soraya, I even thought . . ." She shook her head, the words sticking in her throat. She decided to skip spelling out *exactly* what she'd thought. "I mean, it's not like *I've* met anyone."

Soraya shifted gears as she turned into the Heartland driveway, then glanced across at Amy. "Who was that guy you went out to Arizona with?"

"Will Savage," said Amy. "But that was totally different – our relationship never went beyond being friends."

"So you haven't got involved with anyone yet," Soraya concluded. "It's not because you've been hung up on Ty, right?"

"No! No. I've just been enjoying life, enjoying my freedom." For an instant, the image of Flamenco came into Amy's mind – wild and free, unwilling to take on the burden of a saddle and rider. Perhaps she had been a little bit like the Andalusian mare over the last few months. She hadn't wanted anything to tie her down, either.

But that didn't explain how she felt about Heather.

Soraya parked in the driveway and they got out. The kitchen light went on, and Jack peered out of the front door. Then he saw Soraya and held his arms out for a hug.

"Soraya! It's great to see you, honey. I wondered who was pulling up. I wasn't expecting Amy back for hours."

Soraya hugged him. "I snatched her away from the party," she said. "It's great to see you, too, Mr. Bartlett."

"Well, come on in out of the cold," Jack urged them, leading the way back into the house. "I was just off to bed so I'll leave the two of you to catch up. I expect you've got plenty to talk about."

"We do," said Amy. "But won't you have some hot chocolate with us first, Grandpa?"

Jack cocked his head to one side. "That's a nice idea," he said. "You go get comfortable in the living room while I heat up some milk."

The two girls settled on to sofas in the living room and opened a bag of tortilla chips. Jack came in a few minutes later with three steaming mugs of hot chocolate and sat with them as Soraya told tales of life in her theatre programme. If Jack sensed that anything was amiss, he didn't let on. He never asked what had happened to Ty or what the party had been like, and Amy was grateful. A single image played again and again in her mind like a scene from a bad movie: Ty, bending down towards Heather and laughing as she reached up to kiss him. . .

Once Jack went to bed, Soraya tucked her feet under her in the armchair and got serious. "So," she said, "how are you feeling?"

Amy made a face. "What d'you think?" She spread her arms wide. "Furious, humiliated, confused . . . and about a million other things!"

"Confused? Why confused?"

Amy let her hands fall on to the arms of the sofa. She wasn't sure how to answer that question.

Soraya's expression was shrewd. "Amy, were you hoping that you and Ty would get together again?"

"No! I wasn't. At least, I didn't think–" She lapsed into silence. Soraya reached for another handful of tortilla chips and waited, while Amy hunted carefully for the right words. "I didn't come home expecting anything. I don't know why I feel like this. All I know is, I don't know why he didn't tell me. . ."

"What's she like?" asked Soraya.

"What's who like? Heather?"

"Who else?"

A stream of images flooded Amy's mind: Heather's pretty face, her sparkling blue eyes, her smooth blonde hair, her little strappy top.

"She's cute," she said flatly. "I mean, why wouldn't Ty want to date someone who's petite and blonde and from what I can tell, utterly charming. . . ?"

"Enough!" Soraya ordered. "I didn't ask you about her so you could torture yourself. She sounds hard to hate, though, which could be a problem."

Amy laughed genuinely for the first time since Soraya had picked her up. "I don't want to hate Heather – honestly," she added when her friend raised her eyebrows. "It would make things super-awkward here since she seems to ride Sundance pretty regularly. I just hope Ty doesn't hope we're going to be new best friends by New Year's. I'm not doing that just to make him feel better."

"Feel better about what?" Soraya questioned her. "You're the one that ended the relationship. Why would he think you'd be hurt by him moving on?"

"I'm not –" Amy began, then stopped herself.

"Don't give yourself such a hard time about it," Soraya chided her. "It's completely understandable. You were so close before you left, totally joined at the hip – much closer than Matt and I ever were. You get back after not seeing him for months and, hey, presto, you're close all over again. So you begin to wonder why you split up in the first place. And you probably won't know the answer until you head back to your new life at college."

Amy thought about it. Sitting by a log fire at Heartland, having a heart-to-heart with Soraya, life at college seemed a million miles away. Of course, that life was totally absorbing and, when she was there, she rarely felt sad for the things she was missing at Heartland. In a few weeks, she'd be back there with the group of friends she'd made, working hard and having fun. But when she was at Heartland, it seemed like it was the only place in her life. It was the old Amy who came out here, with all the same relationships and all the same expectations. . .

Soraya was right. *Of course* she was hurt.

Chapter Nine

For the first time since she'd arrived home, the grey light of morning was already filtering through her curtains when Amy woke up. She pushed aside the drapes and looked for a moment at the clear December sky. Only two more days before Christmas Eve – and it was like she could feel the holiday approaching. She sat up with a start and looked at her clock. Seven-thirty! Horrified, she jumped out of bed and tugged on her jeans, as fragments from the night before came together in her head. They had stayed up talking so late that Soraya had decided to stay over in Lou's old room. Amy pulled a fleece over her head, then tiptoed out into the hall. She opened the door of Lou's room and peeked inside. Soraya's dark curls were spread across the pillow – she was still fast asleep.

Amy shut the door again and headed downstairs. Her heart sank at the thought of seeing Ty. In the cold light of day, she realized how much had changed since they had shared the evening chores the night before.

Ty's pickup was already in the front yard. Amy found the barn empty except for Apollo, Red, and Flamenco, and guessed Ty must be turning out the last of the other horses. A quick inspection of the stalls showed he'd started the mucking out, too. Amy took a deep breath. She could do this. She'd ignore the whole thing. She'd say hello to him as though nothing had happened. There was *no way* she'd let on how disappointed, stupid, and humiliated she was feeling. Plodding out to get a wheelbarrow, she tried to shake off the sleepiness that had followed her from her bed. She and Soraya must have talked until three in the morning and Amy's sleep had been restless all night. She started scooping up soiled straw with a pitchfork and dumping it in the wheelbarrow, focusing entirely on the job at hand.

The creak of the barn door made her jump. "Amy?"

To her relief, it was Soraya. "I'm here," Amy said, looking over Jake's half door. "You were fast asleep ten minutes ago."

Soraya yawned and rubbed her eyes. "Tell me about it. I don't know how you guys get up this early every morning."

Amy smiled wanly. "This is late," she said. "We're usually finished with the yard chores by now."

"Give me drama school any day," moaned Soraya. "But hey, I'm up now." Then she lowered her voice. "Have you seen Ty yet?"

Amy shook her head. "I think he's out in the paddocks."

"Well, I can stick around for a little while, if that would make things easier. Have you got another pitchfork? I'll give you a hand."

"Thanks, Soraya." Amy felt a rush of gratitude. It would make things a lot easier having a friend around. "If you're sure."

"Of course I am," said Soraya. "On one condition: we go for a ride later on Jasmine and Sundance. For old times' sake."

"It's a deal. I need to work with Flamenco first, though." Amy let herself out of the stall. "You know, the chestnut I told you about last night. You could go say hello while I get you a pitchfork – she's at the other end of the barn."

"Sure. I'm dying to see you work with her. She sounds amazing."

Soraya wandered down the aisle and Amy headed outside. She knew she was bound to bump into Ty sooner or later, and sure enough, she spotted his tall figure heading into the tack room. She hesitated. That was where the pitchforks were kept. *Don't be ridiculous,* she told herself.

She walked up to the yard and stood at the tack

room door.

"Morning, Ty," she said. "Sorry I overslept."

Ty was replacing a halter on one of the hooks, and he looked around, startled. "Oh – uh, hi, Amy. That's OK."

"Soraya and I are just finishing the mucking out," said Amy, speaking more rapidly than usual. "I'm here to get another pitchfork."

"Fine," said Ty, running a hand through his hair. "Look–"

Amy didn't give him a chance to finish. "When we're finished, I thought I'd work with Flamenco. Is that OK with you?" She marched over and picked up a pitchfork, avoiding Ty's gaze.

"Sure." Ty's voice was cooler. "I'll go muck out the far paddock. It hasn't been done for a few days. Then I'll meet you at the school ring with Flamenco."

"Right. See you down there." Amy tried to make herself sound nonchalant, but she knew it hadn't worked. She walked back down to the barn feeling embarrassed and frustrated. She couldn't bear the thought that Ty was worried about how she might be feeling. After all, nothing had happened between them since she'd gotten back. The only real clue she'd given to her expectations was what she'd said to Chesman, so she'd just have to hope that he hadn't repeated it to Ty.

Her cheeks flushed as she realized the truth: that somewhere in the back of her mind, she had believed that Ty would always be hers; that whatever she did and wherever she went, he would still love her more than he loved anyone else. Ty, Heartland, Jack, the horses: they were all supposed to stay the same, the part of her life that she could come back to. And that was the way she'd been thinking ever since she got home.

While Amy and Soraya finished mucking out the stalls, Flamenco became more and more impatient, banging the door of her stall and whinnying to be let out.

"She sure seems to hate being cooped up," commented Soraya. "She was really curious when I went to say hello, but she got antsy as soon as she realized I wasn't there to take her out."

"She's like a caged tiger," Amy agreed. "We've been turning her out with some of the other horses for the last couple of days, so I guess she felt gypped when Ty took the others out and left her here."

"Did you see Ty when you went outside just now?" Soraya asked.

Amy raised one eyebrow and nodded. "Yup."

"Ah. So I take it things are not exactly relaxed?"

"You could say that. I can tell he's walking on eggshells around me, like he's just waiting for me to explode or break down or show some sign of freaking out. But there's no way I'd do that in front of him."

"Nope," said Soraya. "A girl has to have her pride."

"She sure does." Amy picked up the wheelbarrow. "I said we'd meet him down at the school ring with Flamenco. I just hope all this stuff between us doesn't affect her too badly. She's bound to pick up on it if we're tense."

Soraya held the barn door open for Amy as she pushed the wheelbarrow to the muck heap. Then she went back inside and approached Flamenco's stall, the chestnut mare let out a high-pitched whinny.

"OK, girl," Amy soothed her. "You're coming out now."

She entered the stall and patted Flamenco's neck before clipping a lead rope to her halter. For once, the mare stood still, as if she realized this was part of the routine that led to her being outside.

"That's it. Good girl," Amy praised her, leading her towards the barn door.

Flamenco pranced across the yard, snorting dramatically at the wheelbarrow, her whole body electric as Amy led her down to the school.

"She's beautiful," breathed Soraya, walking by Amy's side. "She's pretty excited, huh?"

"Wait till she's loose," said Amy. "Then you'll see a real show! I'm going to try joining up again, but she might need a little more time before she's ready to trust me."

"Can't wait!" said Soraya.

There was no sign of Ty, so Amy led the mare into the centre of the school and unclipped the lead rope. Exactly as she had predicted, the mare leaped away and galloped to the end of the ring, throwing in some playful bucks. There were some jumps stacked against the railings and Flamenco peered at them suspiciously, then set off again. Amy watched her, wondering where Ty had gone. She knew that he should be in on the session, but all the same, part of her was relieved to be working on her own. Flamenco had already been more responsive this morning; it might be best to keep things simple.

The mare's first burst of energy seemed to be burning out, so Amy moved towards her to drive her around the ring. As she did, she caught sight of Ty walking down the path from the yard. But not just Ty. There were three people altogether. Amy's heart sank. The other two were the Breakspears.

She didn't know whether to run over and make sure

that they didn't interfere with the session, or to focus on Flamenco and hope that Ty and Soraya would keep the visitors occupied. Flamenco made the decision for her. The mare saw her owners and whinnied loudly, veering across the school towards them. In a flash, Amy knew she had to act. She had to make Flamenco pay attention to her or the whole session would be wasted.

"Hey!" she called, and ran at the mare, driving her away from the gate and around the ring again. In one sense, it was good that Flamenco had responded to the Breakspears – it showed that she saw them as familiar, even as friends. But until she learned to join up and trust the humans around her, nothing about her behaviour would change. She might respond while it suited her, but she would still be essentially wild, challenging every effort they made to control her. Out of the corner of her eye, Amy saw Julia's look of horror as Flamenco lowered her head and bucked, but she decided she simply had to shut her audience out. Taking a deep, determined breath, she drove Flamenco on again.

As Amy kept up the pressure, making the mare constantly aware of her presence, she began to see the first signs that Flamenco was starting to respond. The mare was no longer thinking about her owners standing at the gate. She wasn't thinking about her freedom to gallop around the ring. She was focused on Amy, and Amy alone. If Amy moved towards her, she sped up; if she backed off, Flamenco slowed down, watching her curiously to see what she would do next. At last, they were beginning to communicate. And it looked as though the mare might be almost ready to make that crucial step of trust. But Amy wasn't going to let her stop until the signs were clear.

After a few more circuits of the ring, she began to see the signs she was looking for. Flamenco lowered her head in submission and began to chew the air, in exactly the same way that a young horse asks for acceptance within a herd. Her pace had slowed so much that Amy could tell that she was ready to stop, given half the chance. But she had to be sure. She drove the horse around the ring one last time.

Then she stopped and slowly turned her back on the horse. As she did, she became aware that no one at the gate was talking. Everyone's eyes were on her and on Flamenco. Amy stood still, listening for the sound of the mare's footfalls behind her.

The seconds ticked by, and Amy's heart thumped painfully in her chest. She hoped she'd picked the right moment to give the mare a choice – the choice to defend her isolated freedom, or to put her trust in the human in the centre of the ring. Amy knew that for Flamenco, perhaps more than for any other horse she'd worked with, this was a major, life-changing decision that would lead her down a completely different path.

A murmur from the direction of the gate told Amy that the incredible was happening. Flamenco was walking towards her, and now she could hear the mare's soft footfalls on the sandy surface of the ring. A few seconds later, she felt Flamenco's breath on her neck and a velvety muzzle nudged her shoulder. Amy's heart gave a leap of joy.

She smiled, but she didn't move right away. The last thing she wanted to do was startle the mare and undo all this good work. When Flamenco began to butt her arm more demandingly, Amy turned around to face her.

"Good girl," she murmured, gazing into the mare's big brown eyes. The wildness was gone, and Amy felt humbled that she had been able to reach beyond it to let the horse communicate trustingly and openly. Of course, the wild streak would come back again before she was fully trained: It would never go away completely. That was the joy of a horse like Flamenco – she would always be full of spirit. But Amy hadn't forced and coerced her into being something she wasn't. In fact, she hadn't placed any expectations on her; she had allowed Flamenco to take trust at her own pace and in her own time. And that had allowed the mare to cross an important threshold.

With her right hand, Amy reached up and stroked the mare's neck – a long, steady stroke to reassure her and make her feel safe. Only then did Amy look across the school to see the reactions of the people standing at the gate.

Chapter Ten

The Breakspears looked spellbound. Soraya was grinning, her face full of admiration, and while Amy avoided Ty's direct gaze, she could tell he was pleased.

Amy glanced up at Flamenco's face again. "Let's go and say hello, shall we?" She knew that for the time being, the mare would follow her wherever she went without needing to be led. She walked towards the gate and sure enough, Flamenco stayed close at her heels, not wanting even a single stride to separate them.

"I've never seen anything like that in my life," Julia declared as they approached. Amy saw that tears were pooling in her eyes, and warmed to the older woman. She knew it must be very strange and humbling, to see her horse bonding so amazingly with someone else.

"You'll be able to go through the same process yourself, later on," she promised, smiling as Julia reached out to stroke Flamenco's nose. The mare whickered a greeting. "It's a really major step for Flamenco. She's very spirited and independent, so her training needs to be adapted to that. She needs to be sure that she can express herself or she quickly starts to feel trapped."

Julia looked thoughtful. "Do you think that's what I've been doing?" she asked. "Making her feel trapped?"

"Well . . ." Amy hunted for the right words. "You're used to horses that respond well to firm, consistent boundaries. Am I right?"

Julia nodded. "Yes. Logris always seemed happiest when he knew exactly what I expected of him."

"So Flamenco must seem very wild by comparison," said Amy. "And that probably led you to focus on control rather than communication."

She glanced at Ty to check that she wasn't going too far and was relieved to see him nodding in agreement.

"It's true," said Julia. She sighed. "I have been worried about controlling her, and the more I try, the harder it seems to get. I was starting to feel as though I just couldn't handle her. That's why we brought her here."

Rick Breakspear put an arm around his wife's shoulders. "And I think we're glad we did, aren't we, honey?"

"Yes." Julia looked at Amy, her eyes sparkling.

"We'll be able to build on what happened today. It's just the first step, but it's a big breakthrough," Amy said. "We'll school Flamenco in a way that allows room for her to express her character, and gives her a chance to shape her own training. I won't be here for long in the New Year, but Ty and Joni will work with you to make sure that you feel comfortable and confident about carrying on her schooling at home."

"Once we've established a few more of the basics, perhaps you'd like to come and be part of the schooling process while Flamenco is still here," Ty added.

Julia's face lit up. "That would be great. I'd be so interested to understand more about your methods."

"Well, it's wonderful that you're willing to find the right approach for Flamenco," said Amy. "A lot of owners would just battle through and break her spirit instead of working with it."

Julia's eyes flew wide open. "Oh, that would be dreadful!"

"You'd be surprised at how many people try it." Ty leaned to open the gate of the school. "We'll get Flamenco rubbed down now, then turn her out as a reward for responding so well."

Amy clipped the lead rope back on to Flamenco's halter, then handed it to Julia. It was a poignant moment. Fresh from her experience of the join-up, the mare looked around for Amy, unwilling to move from her side. Hastily, Amy moved to the other side of her head so that both she and Julia were close to her.

"Thank you," murmured Julia, flashing Amy a warm smile.

Julia helped Amy and Soraya wipe Flamenco down and put her rug on while Ty chatted to Rick and offered to show him the feed room, where Heartland's collection of aromatherapy and Bach Flower Remedies were kept. Julia asked about Heartland's history, and Amy gave her a brief outline of her parents' lives – how they had both been successful showjumpers in England until an accident had ended her father's career; how they had split up; and how Marion had come back to Virginia to live with her father, Jack, and establish Heartland. Julia listened intently, occasionally asking questions, and Amy realized that she was a sensitive, intuitive woman who was going to be the perfect owner for Flamenco.

"I heard what happened to your mother," Julia said. "Or at least, I heard she died. It's wonderful how you all keep Heartland going."

"Thank you," Amy said quietly. She lifted the heavy New Zealand rug into position, and Julia began to buckle the straps. "It's a pleasure to work with a horse like Flamenco. She has so much to give. It makes everything we do here feel worthwhile."

"All the same, it must be hard for you," said Julia. "You

get to build a wonderful relationship with a horse, and then you have to let it go."

It was an insightful comment. "It can be difficult," Amy admitted. "But it's always rewarding to see a horse reunited happily with its owner."

But as they led the chestnut mare down to the paddock, Amy reflected that it wasn't just the horses that she had to let go. As she'd discovered last night, sometimes it was the people, too. . .

"Race you!" Soraya called over her shoulder, urging Jasmine up the track.

Amy grinned and pushed Sundance on. She knew the dun pony was more than a match for Jasmine any day, and sure enough, he soon drew up alongside the other two. The ponies raced neck and neck but just before the trail narrowed, Sundance pulled ahead. The girls reined them back to a trot, laughing. They'd had lunch, and now they were riding along the familiar trails that led around Teak's Hill.

"That was so much fun," gasped Soraya. "We haven't done that for. . ."

"Over a year," Amy finished for her as they slowed to a walk. "We haven't ridden together since before we went to college." She gave the left rein a tug as Sundance lunged to nip Jasmine's neck. "Stop that!" she scolded

"And Sundance hasn't changed a bit!" said Soraya. "Look at him. He's so grumpy."

Sundance's ears were pinned back, and Amy had to keep a firm grip on the left rein to keep him from veering towards Jasmine.

"He'll always be Heartland's naughtiest pony." Amy patted his neck. "But Heather gets along really well with him."

Soraya looked at her. "Does she?"

Amy nodded and glanced down at her legs. They reached below Sundance's belly. "She's the right size for him, too."

"Ouch."

"Tell me about it. Not that I mind other people riding him," Amy added hastily. "It just feels weird to think of her and Ty coming up here on romantic trail rides together."

"I can't see Sundance giving anyone a chance for romance," Soraya remarked with a chuckle. More seriously, she added, "Did Ty say anything to you today? About Heather, I mean?"

Amy shook her head. "I didn't give him a chance." She

frowned, thinking of their encounter in the tack room. "I was so determined not to let anything show. I just kind of gave him the cold shoulder."

"That seems fair," said Soraya. "He should have told you about Heather ages ago."

"I know," Amy agreed, nudging Sundance forward into a trot again. But as they rode on through the forest, a sudden thought occurred to her. It wasn't just Ty who'd kept things quiet. No one else had mentioned Heather, either – not even Lou. After all these months, it couldn't have been a secret. Then, in an instant, she realized that it wasn't. Scraps of conversation drifted back. . . *It's great that Ty's found someone who's such a big help. . . It's good to know that you two will always get along, no matter how much your lives change. . .* Grandpa and Lou both knew perfectly well. Amy wouldn't have expected Grandpa to tell her, but what about her *sister*? Amy felt a flash of annoyance.

They reached a stretch where fallen branches made perfect jumps for popping over. Sundance leaped over them all with feet to spare.

"He's still got so much bounce in him," commented Amy when they'd finally had enough. "It's such a shame he doesn't get to compete any more." She patted his neck. "I wonder whether Spindle will turn out to be a jumper. He's certainly got the build for it."

But the truth was, she mused as they turned for home, she wouldn't be riding Spindle regularly for another three years – and even then, only if she returned to Heartland for good.

"I'd better head home when we get back," said Soraya, cutting into her thoughts. "I was wondering – are you free to come over for dinner tonight? My mom's cooking up a feast and I know she'd love to see you."

"Sounds lovely," said Amy. "I need to check if someone else can do the evening chores, though." Although she didn't say so, she liked the idea of avoiding Ty for a little longer.

They trotted into the Heartland yard, and Amy jumped down from her pony's back. Lou's car was in the driveway, and so was Nancy's.

"That's hopeful," said Amy to Soraya gesturing at the cars. "It look's like everyone's here, so there's a good chance I'll be able to get away."

"I'll untack the ponies if you want to go and find out," offered Soraya. "They go straight into the barn now, right?"

Amy nodded, handing her reins over. "Thanks. Their rugs are hanging over the stall doors. I won't be long."

She headed into the kitchen and found Nancy balancing a squirming Holly on her knee while Lou leafed through some paperwork at the table. "Hi," Amy greeted them.

Lou glanced up and smiled. "Hi, Amy. Good ride?"

"Amazing. Sundance is doing really well," replied Amy, looking hard at her sister. Would she mention the fact that Ty's girlfriend had been riding him regularly?

Lou didn't take the bait. "It must be great to catch up with Soraya," she said. Then her eyes fell back to the papers in front of her.

Amy wondered whether to mention Heather outright, but it was difficult with Nancy sitting there. She decided to wait for a better moment. "Yeah, it's great to see her. Actually, Lou, I've got a favour to ask you. I'm invited over for dinner at Soraya's tonight. Do you think you could give Ty a hand with the evening chores?"

A frown flickered across Lou's forehead, and she exchanged glances with Nancy. "Well . . . I'm not sure. . ."

There was a pause, and Lou looked awkward.

"I could look after Holly for an hour or two," Nancy offered. "Would that help?"

"But I thought you said you had things to do at home?" Lou asked her.

"Oh, don't worry about that. It's nothing that can't wait."

Lou turned to Amy. "I guess that's a yes, then," she said.

Amy smiled. "That's great. Thanks, Nancy. I'll go tell Soraya."

The next morning, Amy got up early. It seemed particularly cold and she put on an extra thermal T-shirt under her usual shirt and fleece. Then she bounded downstairs – with any luck, she'd have most of the chores done before Ty arrived. It wasn't that she was *avoiding* him exactly. It was just that she couldn't figure out how to act around him now that she knew he was dating someone else – and had been the whole time she'd thought she felt their old spark returning. Which meant she'd seriously misread some signals – or maybe it had been wishful thinking? Whatever it was, she figured it would be easier not to see too much of each other for now.

For the first time, Flamenco greeted her eagerly as she walked into the barn. It was a sure sign that the join-up had had a big effect on the mare, and Amy went straight over to stroke her neck.

"You're getting a rest day today, did you know that?"

she told the mare. "But we'll do some more work together soon, I promise."

As dawn broke and morning light filtered into the yard, Amy surveyed the skies. They were a deep leaden grey, hanging low. For the first time since she'd come home, she realized it really might snow, and soon. She pulled her coat tight around her as she trudged back to the barn. The horses seemed to sense a change in the atmosphere, too, and were quieter than usual as she led them out to the paddocks in pairs.

By the time Ty's pickup pulled into the driveway, Amy had finished the mucking out. Her hands and nose were frozen and she decided to head indoors for a hot cup of coffee.

To her surprise, Nancy was there. She was sitting at the table while Grandpa was making coffee.

"As far as I'm concerned, that's not the problem, Jack–" Nancy stopped abruptly when she saw Amy and quickly dropped her eyes to her lap.

"Is everything OK?" Amy asked.

"Fine, fine," said Nancy in a business-like voice. "Come in out of the cold. You must be frozen. It's dreadful out there this morning."

"Looks like I might need that salt after all," joked

Grandpa. But Nancy didn't smile.

"The horses can tell there's snow in the air," said Amy, stamping her feet. "They're all huddling together in the paddocks already."

Nancy stood up, and began to pull on her coat. "Well, I'd better get moving," she said. "I want to get into town before the roads are all iced up. I have to get a bunch of things from the stores for tomorrow's open house."

"You're not going already!" Jack protested. "You just got here. And I just made coffee."

"Amy can drink the coffee. She needs it more than I do," Nancy replied. "I'll speak to you later, Jack." She blew them both a kiss and disappeared out the front door.

"Well, I guess she's right, honey. Your face is still pink from the cold," Jack said to Amy. He poured her a steaming cup of coffee. "Here you go."

Amy wrapped her hands gratefully around the mug. She had an uneasy feeling that she'd just interrupted an argument. It was odd for Nancy to arrive so early in the morning, and even odder for her to drive off so soon after arriving.

"Grandpa, is everything *really* OK?" she asked cautiously.

"Yes, yes. Why shouldn't it be?"

"Well, I don't know," said Amy. "I just get the feeling that maybe. . ." She trailed off. She didn't like to pry, and Grandpa and Nancy were so much older that asking about their relationship seemed all wrong somehow – almost disrespectful.

"You mustn't worry," Jack said firmly. He went to the door and pulled on his big winter jacket and a thick woolly hat. "I'm going to take a look at that salt. You get nice and warm before you head outside again. I don't want anyone getting sick the day before Christmas Eve."

"OK, Grandpa." Amy smiled at him. "There's no need to worry about me."

She sat, sipping her coffee, browsing through a newspaper that was left on the table when she heard a car pull up. Amy guessed it must be Lou. Sure enough, a few moments later her sister walked through the door carrying Holly, who was bundled in a cute, pink, furry, hooded coat.

"Hi, Amy!" Lou greeted her. "I can't *believe* how cold it is today! Did you have a nice time at dinner last night?"

"Great, thanks. Soraya's mom cooked up a storm." Amy stood up and reached for the coffee pot. "Grandpa just made this. D'you want some?"

"You bet." Lou sat Holly in her high chair while she

took off her coat and gloves. Then she sat down at the table and looked at the open newspaper. "Nancy's been here already?"

Amy put a cup of coffee in front of her. "Yup. She left about ten minutes ago."

Lou frowned. "She left already? Well, I guess she's busy with Christmas stuff."

"Too busy, if you ask me," Amy said meaningfully. "She always seems to be dashing off somewhere. Grandpa's been here on his own a lot since I got back."

"Really?" Lou looked surprised.

Amy sat down next to her sister again. "Actually, I was wondering if there's something wrong."

"Wrong? How so? You know what it's like at this time of year. Everyone's rushing–"

"Wrong between Nancy and Grandpa."

Lou shook her head. "I haven't noticed anything."

Amy gave a wry smile. "Don't tell me," she said casually, "you didn't notice Ty and Heather, either?"

"Ty and Heather? Don't be silly. Of course I knew about that, they've been together for months. . ." Lou's expression changed as Amy held her gaze. "Oh, no. You're not saying. . ." She stopped. "You didn't know?"

"Nope," Amy said quietly. "Why didn't you tell me, Lou?"

Holly reached for the coffee and Lou moved it away from her. "I . . . Amy, I don't know. I just don't know." Her face was stricken. "I guess I just assumed he'd tell you himself. I had no idea. . . When did you find out? You're OK about it, right? I mean, it *was* your decision to break up last spring."

"Yes, it's fine." But then Amy decided to be honest with Lou. "No, it isn't, actually. It was kind of a shock. I only found out when I went to a party and saw Heather kissing him."

"Oh, Amy. I'm so sorry."

Amy rested her chin on her hands. "Well, it's not *your* fault. Ty should have told me," she admitted. "I'm just surprised that no one mentioned it. It was pretty embarrassing – I said all these things at the party and pretty much acted like we were still a couple."

With the coffee out of reach, Holly banged the table in frustration and began to cry. Lou pulled her out of the high chair and sat her on her lap instead. "But I figured that by now you'd be over him," she said, reaching for her bag. "Hang on a minute, Amy. I just need to get Holly something to play with." She pulled a colourful toy out of the bag, a plush dragon with something different to stroke or squeeze at the end of each foot.

Amy waited patiently. She'd forgotten this from the summer – how it was impossible to have a conversation with Lou any more without constant distractions and interruptions. You'd get two sentences in, then Holly would need something or start to cry. Really, it was no wonder Lou hadn't mentioned Heather.

"I *am* over him," Amy said, almost to herself. She shrugged. There was no point in discussing it. "Forget it, Lou. I'm more worried about Grandpa. It would be awful if he and Nancy split up."

"Split up!" Lou was all ears again. "You don't really think that's a possibility, do you?"

"I hope not. She's so totally a part of things now. I've almost forgotten what Heartland was like without her."

"Me, too," said Lou. She smiled wryly. "Even though I went out of my way to make her feel unwelcome at first." She stroked her little girl's hair. "Holly adores her. She's like a great-grandma to you, isn't she?"

Holly squealed and shook the dragon so that a bell rang inside its bright green ear.

"I think they had an argument this morning," Amy went on. "And like I said, Grandpa's been here on his own almost every night since I got back. Maybe we take Nancy too much for granted, Lou."

Guilt flitted across Lou's face. "Maybe. I rely on her a lot these days. She would have left last night if I hadn't asked her to look after Holly. What were they arguing about?"

"I'm not sure," said Amy. "I interrupted something and then she left. Grandpa said there was nothing wrong, but I'm not sure I believe him."

Lou played with the toy dragon for a moment, squeezing one foot so that it made a squeaking noise. Holly giggled in delight and reached for the foot every time Lou stopped.

"It would be so hard for Grandpa if he lost Nancy," Lou said. "I don't know what he'd do, living here on his own with no one to help him. He's getting old, Amy."

Amy nodded. Grandpa had been through enough. He'd lost his wife and his daughter. It would just be too cruel if he ended up on his own again. She met Lou's gaze and a ripple of sympathy passed between them. Amy knew that however preoccupied her sister might be, losing someone was something they both understood far too well.

Chapter Eleven

Now that she was finally warm, Amy put her coat back on and braced herself for the cold again. With Flamenco having a rest day, she decided it was a good opportunity to take Spindle out for his first solo trail ride – just a short one, up the ridge and back; it was too cold to be out for long. The morning sky was hardly any lighter than it had been at dawn, and an icy wind was starting to blow.

Amy hurried down to the paddock, jogging to keep herself warm. The horses were still huddled together, barely bothering to graze, and Amy didn't blame them. She made a mental note to bring them all back into the barn after her trail ride and give them each a fat hay net.

In spite of the weather, Spindle was still happy to see her and cantered over to the gate when Amy approached. She led him up to the yard and tacked him up. She realized she should let Ty know where she was going – after all, Spindle was still a young horse, and the weather could turn nasty – so she left a note in the tack room before swinging herself into the saddle.

Spindle was as excited as ever to be out on the trail, and he didn't seem to mind the cold. He willingly broke into a trot when Amy asked him to, and they made their way briskly past the paddocks and up into the woods. Between the trees, the day seemed darker than ever, and before long, Amy noticed the first snowflakes drifting down between the branches and landing on her glove. She pushed the young horse into a canter along a short straight stretch, then began to wonder if she should turn back.

The whine of machinery stopped her. She wasn't far from the lumberyard, and with a flash of guilt, the memory of the dapple grey mare popped back into her mind – and with it, the realization that she'd completely forgotten to call Mr. and Mrs. Hayes, her owners. Ty had given her the number just before inviting her to the party and she'd meant to make the call the next day. It seemed an eternity ago. Shaking her head at neglecting to follow up on the mare, she turned down the path that led alongside the little field.

At first, the field appeared empty. Then Amy saw the flick of the donkey's tail in the shadows of the shelter, and she realized that they were inside, probably taking shelter from the biting wind. Or at least the donkey was.

She called, wondering if they would respond to her voice. To her relief, the mare's head peered out of the shelter, followed by the donkey's. Spindle whinnied an eager greeting and the donkey trotted over to the fence with the mare lumbering slowly behind him.

Amy studied the mare carefully. Her udder was full, and even from Spindle's back she could see that the muscles around her tail had relaxed even further. She would almost certainly give birth in the next couple of days, but there was no sign that her owners were prepared for it. And now the weather was taking a turn for the worse – possibly much worse. The mare should be in a warm shelter by now, being regularly monitored.

Amy allowed Spindle to touch noses with the shaggy donkey, then turned him around and set off down the trail. She glanced back to see both the mare and the donkey staring after her. A gust of icy wind blew, and Amy's heart contracted. Suddenly, she knew that she wouldn't be able to rest until she knew that these two were being cared for properly.

The snowflakes began to fall more steadily, filling the forest with swirling miniature ghosts. It felt a little warmer, as though a soft blanket was dropping slowly from the sky, but Amy wasn't deceived; the wind was still gusting, and as the afternoon closed in, the temperature would be dropping further. She pushed Spindle into a canter whenever she could, frequently needing to brush the snowflakes out of her eyes, and felt relieved when Heartland's familiar rooftops appeared.

"Good boy, Spindle," she murmured, bringing him back to a walk for the final part of the ride. They clattered into the yard and she jumped off his back.

Ty appeared in the tack room door. "Amy! I was worried about you," he said. "I got your note."

"I'm fine," Amy told him, a little stiffly. "But I'm not so sure about the pregnant mare along the ridge. She's really close to foaling."

"Did you call the Hayes?" asked Ty.

Amy tensed. "No, I didn't," she answered, trying not to let it sound like a snap.

"I'll call them now," she said over her shoulder, leading Spindle down to the barn. "I'll just put Spindle in his stall. I think we should get the other horses in, too."

With Spindle happily munching from his hay net, Amy went back up to the yard with his tack, then fished out her mobile and the number that Ty had given her. She punched it in.

It took several rings before someone answered. At last, a quiet-sounding woman picked up the phone.

"Hello? Is this Mrs. Hayes?" asked Amy.

"Mrs. Hayes? Oh, no, I'm sorry, she's away at the

moment," replied the woman. "This is Susan Cheshire. I'm house-sitting for them. May I take a message?"

"Mrs. Hayes is away?" Amy checked. "And Mr. Hayes isn't there, either?"

"No, they're away until after Christmas. They'll be back on the twenty-seventh." Mrs. Cheshire hesitated. "Who's calling, please?"

"It's Amy Fleming, from Heartland, down in the valley," said Amy. "I spotted the mare in the Hayes's paddock when I was out riding earlier. I'm worried about her – she's very close to giving birth."

"Oh, so that's the problem," said Mrs. Cheshire, sounding reassured. "You don't need to worry about that, dear. Mr. and Mrs. Hayes said Night Owl wouldn't give birth until they got back. Now let me see – I've got her due date written down here – yes, it's January eighth."

Amy creased her forehead in concern. "Well . . . I'm afraid that may not be the case. I'm studying to be a vet and I'd say she could go into labour at any moment. It's not great if that happens without supervision."

"Oh, my goodness. I don't know anything about horses – I just assumed. . ." Mrs. Cheshire sounded thoroughly alarmed, and Amy felt a twinge of annoyance with the mare's owners. It wasn't right to leave an inexperienced person to deal with a pregnant mare, however unlikely it was that she'd give birth.

"But Reuben's with her," Mrs. Cheshire carried on. "That helps, doesn't it?"

"Reuben?"

"The donkey."

Amy bit back a sarcastic comment. None of this was Mrs. Cheshire's fault, she reminded herself. "Well, he's good company for her, of course," she said in as light a tone as possible. "But if she gets into trouble giving birth, he won't be much help, I'm afraid."

"Of course not. How silly of me." Mrs. Cheshire sounded very flustered now. "So what should I do?"

"Hmm." Amy was considering the situation when Ty appeared in the tack room doorway. "Well, we're reasonably close, so we can check on her again. We can't offer twenty-four-hour attention, but at least we'd be able to call a vet if she runs into problems."

"Oh, if you could, I'd be so grateful," said Mrs. Cheshire, sounding relieved. "If there's anything I can do. . ."

"We'll let you know," Amy assured her. She flipped the phone shut, thinking hard. "We'd better get up there before the snow gets any worse," she said, turning to Ty.

It seemed strange that the mare's due date was so far

ahead, especially when she was so big. Amy thought back to the mare's appearance, picturing her swollen belly in her mind. Could there be another explanation, she wondered? It couldn't be . . . *twins*? She dismissed the thought. Equine twins were incredibly rare.

"I think we need to get moving," said Ty, cutting into her thoughts.

"Yes." Amy peered out of the tack room as a gust of wind blew a flurry of snowflakes into the doorway. "But we'd better get our own horses in first."

They trudged out into the yard, the wind lashing the snow into their faces. If there wasn't so much to do, Amy would have found it exciting – there was always something wonderful about the winter's first snowfall.

The horses were standing with their backs to the wind, their tails tucked low between their legs. They were all too willing to be led up to the barn and out of the wind and cold. With their New Zealand rugs exchanged for dry stable rugs and a big hay net each, they all looked much more relaxed, and the barn began to fill with their warmth. As she delivered the last hay net to Jake's stall, Amy felt warmer inside, too. She listened to the munching of hay and the rustle of fresh mouthfuls being pulled from the nets, and smiled.

Ty was waiting for her in the front yard. "I think we should take Jack's pickup," he said. "We're going to need four-wheel drive, so mine's no good."

"Did you ask him?" asked Amy.

"Yes, he said to go right ahead," said Ty. "He's using the tractor to salt the driveway."

"OK, let's go."

The wind was driving the snow into a blizzard as they battled across the yard and into the cab of the pickup. They slowly set off along the dirt road that led around the bottom of the ridge. Ty peered through the windshield; the wipers were barely managing to brush aside the drifting snow.

Amy stared ahead, her knuckles white as they gripped the sides of her seat. Driving in a storm was her worst nightmare; that was how her mother had been killed. Ty concentrated on driving and a silence settled over the cab.

The edge of the field came into view and Amy peered at it, puzzled. Something had changed. She squinted to see through the snow, trying to work out why the field looked different.

"What happened?" she exclaimed. "I can't even see the shelter any more."

"Must be the snow," said Ty.

"It can't be." Amy narrowed her eyes against the blinding white to make sense of the rearranged shapes.

Even before Ty brought the pickup to a halt, Amy was clambering out, jumping down on to the snowy ground and running towards the field. Once closer to the fence, her heart gave a sickening lurch. The pine tree that had stood next to the shelter had been blown over by the wind, and had come crashing down into the field.

Amy closed her eyes for a second. A fallen tree . . . *a fallen tree.* She pushed aside the memory of that other tree, the tree that had robbed her of so much. She forced herself to open her eyes again and look more closely.

The tree had missed the shelter itself, but its branches were blocking the entrance. Amy bit her lip. Where was Night Owl? And Reuben? Her heart pounding, she climbed over the fence, dreading what she might find in the gloomy depths of the shelter. Pushing twigs and branches to one side, she tried to see inside, but it was hopeless.

"I've got a flashlight!" Ty called, waving it in his hand as he climbed over the fence. He jumped down and ran over to Amy.

As he did, a furry brown face appeared around the side of the shelter.

"Reuben!" cried Amy. "Ty, he's outside!"

She scrambled through the topmost branches of the tree to approach the shelter from the side, and there, to her immense relief, stood both Night Owl and Reuben, hiding from the worst of the wind and snow.

"Oh, thank goodness," Amy gasped as Ty trampled through the branches after her. "They weren't inside the shelter when the tree fell."

"Is either of them hurt?"

Amy pushed aside the last of the branches and stepped free of the tree. Slowly, so as not to startle her, she approached Night Owl. Reuben barged in front of her begging for attention, and Amy stroked his furry neck. The donkey seemed perfectly fine, but she was worried about the mare. She was a lot more subdued than her friendly companion.

"She's not in labour, is she?" asked Ty.

Amy moved around to the mare's side to take a good look at her, bending down to peer at the udder underneath the huge belly. Night Owl wasn't showing obvious signs of discomfort, but her udder was full. "It's hard to tell. No mare is exactly the same. She's standing very still, so I don't think anything's going to happen just yet."

"And she's not injured?" Ty kept his distance as Amy

stroked the mare's neck, reassuring her.

"No. I guess she would have been distressed by the tree falling, but I can't see any signs of it having hit her." She worked her way along the mare's body again, feeling her belly, then gently lifting her tail to check what stage she was at. The muscles around the tail were soft and relaxed, just as they had been before. The mare's time was close, but *how* close?

Amy looked around. There was no way they could move the tree away from the entrance to the shelter. But Night Owl couldn't give birth out in the blizzard.

"Ty, we have to move them," she said. "It's risky – I don't like to do it at this late stage. But we have to try."

Ty brushed snow from his eyebrows and frowned. "Well, the closest buildings are up at the lumberyard. It might be too much for her to get her to all the way to Heartland," he said.

Amy's heart sank. Going up to the Middletons' place was the last thing on earth that she wanted to do right now. But as a gust of wind blew a flurry of snow into her eyes, she knew she had to forget her own feelings. Night Owl and Reuben were all that mattered. "OK," she said. "Maybe you could call someone and check it out?"

Ty fished in his pocket for his mobile. "The lumberyard

closed for Christmas at lunchtime today," he said, his fingers fumbling from the cold. "There won't be anyone there. I'll try Heather."

Amy found some horse cookies in her coat pocket and fed them to the mare. Reuben crowded in, butting her hand as Night Owl lipped them up. "Don't worry, I'll find some for you, too," she promised, dipping into her pocket again. Reuben munched them up, then nudged her elbow, demanding more.

"That's all I've got," Amy told him, glancing at Ty to see if he'd finished his phone call.

He was just winding up. "That's fine. There's a small barn at the back of the yard that isn't being used. Heather says she'll meet up with us there with some feed and straw. I said that hay would be enough at this point – is that OK? Night Owl doesn't need anything else, does she?"

Amy shook her head, concentrating on everything she'd learned about foaling. "No, she won't need any rich feed until after she's given birth," she said. "It could give her constipation."

"Is she really that close?" Ty looked anxious. "Do you think we'll be able to get her up there in time?"

"She hasn't started waxing yet," said Amy. "That's when sticky droplets of milk start oozing from the teats, and it usually happens just before labour starts. I think we're OK." She reached for the mare's forelock. "Come on, girl. We've got to get you up the hill."

Reluctantly, the mare shifted her weight forward in response to Amy's gentle tug. "That's it, good girl," Amy encouraged her.

Ty led the way, pushing aside the twigs as they skirted the top of the fallen tree. Amy glanced back at Reuben, but there was no need to worry about him – he had no intention of being left behind. She gave her full attention to Night Owl, who picked her way carefully as they headed towards the fence.

The fence. The realization dawned on Amy: It was a *fence* – there was no *gate*. "Ty!" she called. "How are we going to get over?"

Ty half turned. "I'll check Jack's pickup for tools," he said. "We'll just have to take a section down. You stay here, I won't be long."

Amy nodded and watched him stride off, his shoulders hunched against the falling snow. The flakes were so thick that by the time he had clambered over the fence, she could barely see him. She stroked Night Owl's ears and stamped her feet. Reuben nudged her elbow again, and she put an arm around his neck, glad of his furry warmth. She sure hoped there were some tools in the pickup.

By the time Ty's figure emerged from the snow again, she was beginning to shiver. Melted snow, blown by the wind, had managed to trickle down inside her clothes, and her feet felt like blocks of ice. But when Ty waved a mallet and a claw hammer at her, she managed a stiff, frozen smile of relief.

"These'll do it!" he called. "It'll only take a few minutes."

With a few well-aimed knocks of the mallet, he loosened the rails from the nearest post, and pulled out the nails with the claw hammer. A gap opened up, and Amy led the mare forward again.

"Not far," she whispered as they began to take slow, steady steps up the slope towards the lumberyard. She placed her hand behind the mare's foreleg to feel for her heartbeat, and was reassured to find that it was normal. "Come on. You can do it, Night Owl!"

Chapter Twelve

With her head bent down against the wind and snow, and all her concentration focused on the mare, Amy didn't think about how far it was to the lumberyard, or what they would find there when they arrived. All she could do was urge Night Owl to take one step after another up the slope. At last, she looked up and realized that they were almost there. Her heart filled with relief.

A figure appeared in the snow and beckoned them forward.

"It's this way!" called Heather's voice.

Amy placed her hand on Night Owl's neck and squinted at the buildings that were just visible ahead. With snow driving across the deserted parking lot, the lumberyard was barely recognizable; the big Christmas tree looked like any other fir tree with its twinkling lights turned off. The little party plodded across the yard until suddenly, as they stepped between two of the big barns, the storm seemed to cease. Amy knew it hadn't – it was just that they were sheltered from the wind – but it made her realize what hard work it had been to battle against the weather as they'd climbed the slope.

Heather was pink-cheeked beneath her cosy knitted hat. "The little barn's through here," she said. "We're almost there."

The friendliness that she'd shown on the night of the party was gone, replaced by something close to coolness. Amy couldn't help wondering what Ty had said to her. She threw a glance over her shoulder and found that Ty was ushering Reuben along from behind, his expression unreadable. Amy felt irritated. There'd be none of this awkwardness if he'd had the guts to tell her about Heather in the first place.

Night Owl's head was drooping, her sides heaving, but Amy was sure she could manage the few final steps. She patted the mare's neck and gently pulled her onward. The barn was really a brick storage shed. It had just one little window at the back, and two or three panes of corrugated clear plastic in the roof, but these were already coated in snow. Some light filtered in, but overall the space was gloomy.

Ty flicked his flashlight on, and Amy saw that Heather had been hard at work. The floor was covered with a thick layer of straw and a hay net was hanging from a hook in one corner. Reuben made his way straight over to it. Night Owl wasn't interested in the food. She stepped on to the straw, then sank to her knees in exhaustion, flopping her whole distended body down to the floor.

"Is she OK?" Heather asked, sounding alarmed.

Amy knelt down beside the mare and examined her. "She needs to rest," she said. "And she needs some water. Is there a bucket we could use?"

"Sure." Heather darted out of the barn, and Amy continued her check, beginning with the mare's lower eyelids for signs of anaemia, and continuing along her body for evidence of labour. To her relief, there were no signs of either. What the mare needed was peace and quiet, and the chance to regain some strength before giving birth.

Now that her eyes had adjusted to the light, Amy looked around. Although it was dark, the shed was cosy and a lot warmer than she'd hoped. The howling blizzard outside couldn't touch Night Owl and Reuben here.

Heather came back with a bucket of water, and Amy offered it to the mare where she lay on the straw. Night Owl drank, sucking up half of it immediately. Then she rested her muzzle on the lip of the bucket, her breathing calmer and her dark eyes full of trust. Amy stroked her ears to warm them, then got up and took the bucket away, placing it near the door.

"Could I have the light, please, Ty?" she asked.

Amy shone it on to the walls and the corners of the barn. If this was where the mare was going to give birth, it had to be free of anything sharp or dangerous for the foal. There was an old rusty nail sticking out from one of the walls, so Ty used the claw hammer to yank it out.

"She's trying to get up," Heather pointed out.

The three of them watched as Night Owl struggled to her feet. Amy studied her for signs that she was entering labour, but the mare didn't seem any more restless. In fact, her ears pricked when she realized that Reuben was pulling on a hay net, and she nudged him to one side to make room for her to eat, too.

"Do you think we can leave her?" asked Ty.

Amy hesitated. In an ideal world, the mare would have someone constantly nearby until the birth. But she hadn't started waxing yet. Although things could start happening at any moment, it could also be days before she gave birth. The best they could do would be to monitor her as often as possible. "I think we'll have to," she said reluctantly. "But we should come back tomorrow."

"I could do that," offered Heather.

Amy shook her head. "There's no need," she said. "I'll come back myself."

Heather glanced at Ty, as if to check what he thought, and Amy felt another twinge of annoyance.

"Amy studied foaling at college," Ty explained. "We'll manage, Heather. The route here over the ridge might be snowed in tomorrow, but we should be able to drive along the road from Heartland. Don't worry."

Heather's face fell. Maybe she wasn't too happy at the thought of Amy working with her boyfriend – but that was just too bad.

"OK, if you're sure." Heather shoved her hands into her coat pockets and looked out at the storm. "I guess I should head back before the snow gets any worse."

Ty looked across at Amy. "That goes for us, too."

Amy watched Night Owl pull a mouthful of hay from the net and nodded. "Yep, we'd better get moving."

"Right," said Heather. "Well, I guess I'll see you tomorrow."

Amy frowned. Hadn't they just said that she didn't need to come?

"The open house at Heartland," Heather explained, shooting Ty a nervous glance.

"Oh! Yes, of course," said Amy. She'd forgotten all about it. It was an annual tradition at Heartland on Christmas Eve – neighbours and friends were all invited to pop by for a glass of mulled wine, cookies, and pie. It hadn't occurred to Amy that Heather would come but she must have been included on the lumberyard invitation. She smiled stiffly. "See you there."

Heather nodded, and Ty put a hand on her shoulder as she turned to head out of the barn. Amy watched him walk her out into the snow, then took a deep breath and checked Night Owl over for the last time. The mare seemed comfortable enough, and butted Amy affectionately. Amy kissed her nose, gave Reuben a hug, then followed Ty and Heather out into the yard.

Heather's truck was just pulling away and Ty came to walk by Amy's side as they began to tramp through the snow in the opposite direction. At least the wind was behind them now, and they made rapid progress down the hill. Ty was subdued, and Amy sensed that he wanted to say something, but she wasn't about to make things easier for him by asking him what.

It was only when they were back in the shelter of the pickup that he spoke. "Amy. . ." He trailed off, then tried again. "Amy, you are OK about Heather, aren't you?"

"Sure," Amy said brightly. She was hardly going to let him think otherwise. "Why shouldn't I be?"

"Well, there's no reason why not, but. . ."

Amy looked out of the window at the falling snow. "Heather seems like a great person, Ty," she heard herself say. "It looks like you're really good together."

"Yeah," said Ty. He seemed relieved. "I think we are." He crunched the gears as they hit a soft patch of snow, then placed his hand lightly on the steering wheel to let the pickup find its own way through it. Once back on firmer ground, he looked across at Amy. "How about you?"

Amy flushed. "What d'you mean, how about me?"

Ty's green eyes met hers. "You must be meeting tons of guys at college. I bet they're all crazy about you."

"Ty!" Amy gave a cracked laugh, but she felt relieved, too. If that's the way he was thinking, it was fine with her. And it didn't look as though Chesman had told him about her creative truth, either. "I'm not seeing anyone, if that's what you mean."

Ty raised an eyebrow and didn't say anything for a moment or two. Then he looked at her again. "I guess that's your choice," he said. "Isn't it?"

Amy thought of Will and of some of the other guys who'd asked her out on dates over the last two terms. It had been fun to have their attention, but she hadn't wanted to get serious with any of them. The truth was, none of them had seemed a match for Ty.

But now she'd have to lay that to rest. "Yes," she said firmly. "It is."

The snowstorm continued for the rest of the afternoon, making it impossible to exercise any of the horses. Ty headed for the tack room to tidy up, and Amy went indoors to call Susan Cheshire and let her know about the fallen tree, and where they had taken Night Owl and Reuben.

Mrs. Cheshire was horrified to hear what had happened and full of gratitude towards Ty and Amy for helping out. "Is there anything I can do?" she said anxiously. "I've been delivering hay to the field in the mornings. Shall I bring some to the lumberyard instead?"

"I'm afraid the road over the ridge may not be passable now, unless you have four-wheel drive," said Amy. "But we can get there to check on Night Owl and take her food from here. If you leave it to us, we can fill in the Hayses when they return."

"Oh, thank you," said Mrs. Cheshire. "I'll let them know."

"A pleasure," Amy told her. "Happy holidays to you."

"And to you, too!" exclaimed Mrs. Cheshire.

Amy put the phone down and went into the kitchen, where Nancy and Lou were in full-scale organizational mode for the open house the next day – Christmas Eve. Nancy was baking mini quiches and sausage rolls, and Lou was weaving a big holly wreath to hang on the front door. Holly was watching the bustling scene from the safety of her baby bouncer.

"The tree's arriving in the morning," Lou announced, winding a wide strip of red ribbon among the sprigs of holly. She glanced out of the window. "At least, I hope it is. We'd better not be snowed in."

"Not a chance. Not with Jack's supply of salt," said Nancy, making Lou and Amy laugh. It was nice to see Nancy looking more relaxed, but the memory of the conversation with Lou stuck in Amy's mind. The kitchen table was piled high with Nancy's baking, and someone had rinsed all the wine glasses and stacked them in the drainer. Nancy again. They'd only ever gotten things ready at the last minute in the past. She made such a huge difference, but most of the time it was barely acknowledged.

Making up her mind to make sure Nancy knew how much she was loved and appreciated in future – if she had the chance – Amy offered to help. Lou gave her a stack of Christmas cards to string up around the house, so she put a CD of Christmas songs on the stereo to work to. With the smell of baking wafting in from the kitchen, snow falling softly outside and familiar tunes ringing through the house, it was difficult not to feel festive.

As the evening began to draw in, Amy realized that the storm was easing up. She went out to help Ty with the evening chores and found that the air was still, with just a few flakes falling. Snow had settled thickly on all the rooftops and drifted up against the corners of the house and stables, but Nancy was right: Jack's salt had kept the driveway clear.

Ty and Amy started changing the water buckets and preparing the evening feeds. When they spoke, it was about practicalities – quantities of bran, or a tear in one of the rugs. In spite of their chat in the car, the distance between them was palpable. Huge gaps had opened up where there used to be laughter and affection. Amy thought about how it had felt when she'd first arrived home from college; now they were back to being strangers again.

"Jack salted both the school rings," said Ty as they walked back to the yard. "So if the snow stops, we should be able to do some exercising tomorrow."

"And we could turn them out, too, as long as another storm doesn't blow in," Amy agreed. She felt like she was on the other end of a phone call, carefully sticking to

Heartland business and staying well away from talking about anything personal. Ty would always be a great colleague, and he had been a great boyfriend, too. Couldn't they find a way to be friends?

They discussed the schedule for the next day: a trip to the lumberyard to check on Night Owl followed by exercise for Red and Apollo, and a session with Flamenco. Then they'd be heading indoors for the open house, and Amy would be seeing Heather yet again.

As Ty climbed into his pickup and headed off, Amy felt like kicking the tack room door in frustration. Treating Ty as just a colleague was so frustrating. She'd always known she was special to him in the past. Was Heartland going to be just where he worked now? She rested her head on the door, her heart full of disbelief. Could all those years of friendship really have melted away so easily?

The next morning dawned bright, crisp, and sunny: a perfect Christmas Eve with the snow hugging the stable rooftops and the sky clear blue above. Ignoring the heavy feeling in her heart, Amy concentrated on practical tasks. She prepared a foaling kit bag for Night Owl, just in case she needed it – at the very least, she would wrap the mare's tail in a bandage this morning, to keep it out of the way. As

Amy and Ty drove up the path towards the lumberyard, the forest looked like the setting for a fairy tale. The conifers were weighed down with soft white cushions, delicate icicles hung from their feathery branches. The new snow didn't make the driving easier, but they managed to make it to the yard without too much trouble.

Amy jumped out and pulled her kit bag and a bale of hay from the back of the pickup, then threw the hay over her shoulder and made her way to the little shed. Her heart was beating faster as she peered inside.

Night Owl was lying down on the straw. Reuben was standing close to her, almost as though he was on guard. As Amy pushed the door open, the mare scrambled to her feet and Reuben let out an earsplitting bray of excitement before heading straight for the bale of hay.

"OK, OK," said Amy. She pushed him gently to one side. "Wait a minute. . ." She put the hay down in one corner, then manoeuvred around Reuben to get to Night Owl.

Starting with her bulging belly, Amy began to examine the mare systematically, first feeling for movement, then looking for signs of labour in her swollen udder and under her tail. Ty appeared in the doorway and filled the hay net with some of the hay while she worked.

Everything was pretty much as it had been the night

before. Night Owl seemed no more restless, and there was still no waxy colostrum gathering on her teats, though her udder was perhaps a little more full. Satisfied that nothing was happening for the time being, Amy took out a clean tail bandage and wrapped the tail. It was good to lose herself in concentrating on the task at hand.

"All done?" asked Ty as she tied the ends in a little knot and tucked it into the bandage.

"I just need to wash her," said Amy. "I'll go get some water." She picked up the bucket that she'd brought as part of the kit. "I'll be right back."

The lumberyard seemed peaceful as Amy walked across it, her feet crunching in the fresh, untouched snow. The only sound was the creaking of pine boughs and the sound of dripping as the morning sun made some of the icicles melt.

The water was ice cold, but it would have to do. Amy half filled the bucket and hurried back, added a little disinfectant and wiped under the mare's tail area. The muscles were very relaxed. It wouldn't be long now.

"She seems comfortable enough," commented Ty, once she'd finished.

"Yes." Amy stepped back and studied the mare as she nosed at the hay net. "There's nothing else I can do right now. I still don't like leaving her, but she's better off here than in the field."

"We can come back later," Ty suggested. "After the open house."

Amy watched as the mare stopped chewing, then peered around uneasily at her belly. The possibility of twins flitted through her mind again. If she *was* carrying two foals, the birth could be very risky, for both the mare and her offspring. If only there was some way they could monitor her constantly! But there wasn't. She and Ty were needed at Heartland.

Coming back later was the best they could do.

Back at Heartland, they set to work separately. Ty rode Apollo in the smaller school ring while Amy lunged Flamenco, then they tacked up Red and Spindle and schooled them, too. With clouds gathering overhead once again, they brought the rest of the horses in before Ty headed off to change for the open house. They'd managed to work together perfectly well, but there was still a chasm between them that nothing seemed to fill.

She went inside for lunch and found the kitchen buzzing: Lou and Nancy were still fussing over the party food, Jack was pulling the newly arrived Christmas tree into the living room, and Scott Trewin, Lou's husband, had arrived just in time to comfort Holly, who had started to cry.

"Amy, do you have time to decorate the Christmas tree?" Lou asked almost as soon as she walked through the door.

Amy leaped at the chance. It would be a great way to forget about Ty and start feeling more festive. "I'd love to!" she responded, pulling off her boots.

"Thanks, that'll be a great help," said Lou, consulting a to-do list on the table. "Now, I think we've got enough pies . . ."

"Never!" Scott joked. "You've only been cooking them for a week!"

"Oh, be quiet," said Lou, grinning at him. "You know you'll eat half of them single-handed."

Scott bounced Holly up and down, making her giggle. "I'll do my best," he promised.

Amy grabbed a couple of mini quiches from the pile that Nancy was arranging and escaped from the mayhem of the kitchen. She loved decorating the Christmas tree, unwrapping the silvery baubles from the tissue paper they'd been sitting in all year, breathing in the aromas of spicy pine needles and metallic tinsel, and finally, when the whole tree was heavily laden, turning on the twinkling lights.

Jack switched on the Christmas carols, which added to the general air of festivity, and Amy set to work, humming along to the music and keeping one ear out for interesting snippets of news from the kitchen. She could tell when Nancy had put the mulled cider on the stove, because the whole house slowly filled with the scent of ginger and cinnamon.

She'd barely finished the tree when the first guests arrived. It was Scott's parents, along with Scott's younger brother, Matt, who had gone to high school with Amy. He gave her an enormous hug.

"So tell me," Matt said, when they'd finished comparing notes on the differences between his premed programme and her vet classes. "Who are you seeing these days?"

Amy shook her head. "I'm not seeing anyone, actually."

Matt raised one eyebrow. "What's going on?" he demanded. "Are all vet students crazy? What are they waiting for?"

"Well . . . it would help if I was interested, I guess," Amy said with a wry smile.

"Ah." Matt gazed at her.

Amy felt her cheeks flush. Matt knew her far too well and she knew exactly what he was conveying with the expression on his face. "No, no." She dismissed him with a wave of her hand. "There's nothing between me and Ty any more. We're just good friends."

"If you say so." He narrowed his eyes. "So what *are* you waiting for, Miss Fleming?"

Amy shrugged. "Just to feel ready," she said simply. "I don't need anyone right now. There's enough happening in my life as it is." She decided to change the subject. "So what about you?"

"Me?" Matt's eyes became mischievous. "Well, to be honest, I think I've met the perfect girl."

"You have?"

Matt grinned. "Yup. Only problem is, she doesn't know it yet."

Amy laughed. "She has no idea?"

"Well, I wouldn't say *that,*" he said, the corners of his mouth twitching. "Let's just say she's playing hard to get. But I've got spies and they assure me that when I ask her out in January, she'll say yes."

"I hope she does. Good luck," said Amy. "I'll be thinking of you."

Out of the corner of her eye, she saw that Ty had arrived with Heather. They were standing at the far end of the living room, holding glasses of cider, talking to Scott. Amy shifted so that she had her back to them. She didn't feel ready to face Heather again just yet.

"I'm going to grab something to drink," she said to Matt. "Can I get you anything?"

Matt shook his head. "No, you go ahead. I'm still half full here." He raised his glass.

"OK," said Amy, and slipped away. She wished Soraya could be there to give her some moral support, but she was picking up Anthony from the airport. Amy took a deep breath. She didn't *have* to speak to Heather. There were plenty of people to speak to – old neighbours and friends, people she hadn't seen for ages. *Anyway,* she scolded herself, *you're an adult now. Now's the time to start behaving like one!*

She found Nancy taking yet another batch of rolls out of the oven.

"Nancy! You can't be stuck out here!" Amy exclaimed. "Here, let me help you with those so you can come in and enjoy the party."

"Don't worry," said Nancy. "It's the last batch."

"But I *do* worry," Amy blurted out before she could stop herself. "You do so much for us here. Sometimes I wonder if you have any time for your own life at all."

"Don't be silly," said Nancy. She got a spatula and began

loosening the rolls from the baking tray. "You know I like to help out."

"Maybe we take that too much for granted," said Amy. "I'm so sorry if we do."

To her surprise, Nancy held the spatula still for a second. Her lip wobbled, and she turned her face away. Then she put the knife down and turned to Amy, her eyes brimming. "That's very sweet of you to say," she said. "And you're right. It isn't easy, becoming part of someone else's family. But you know I adore you all. Don't you?"

"Well, I think so." Amy searched Nancy's face for the reason behind her unexpected bout of emotion.

Nancy smiled and enveloped Amy in a hug. "Well, I do."

"I know we didn't make things easy for you at first," Amy began awkwardly.

Nancy waved her hand dismissively. "Ancient history," she said. "And it couldn't have been easy to see another woman coming to Heartland as if she were trying to fill your mother's place. But you know I wasn't trying to do that." Her blue eyes held Amy's. "Just as I've never expected you and Lou to take Jennifer's place." Nancy's daughter, Jennifer, had died of leukaemia at the age of fifteen; Amy and Lou had only discovered this tragic fact when they met Nancy in the cemetery where their mother was buried.

Impulsively, Amy reached over and wrapped her arms around Nancy, comforting her as she had been comforted before. "Jennifer was so lucky to have you as a mom," she whispered. "And I know my mom would have loved you."

They stayed close for a couple more moments, then pulled apart, sniffing and half laughing. "Look at us!" Nancy exclaimed. "We'll make these rolls soggy if we're not careful. Come on, let's go and feed our hungry guests."

Amy carried a plateful of rolls through to the living room. Looking across the room, she saw Ty's hand on Heather's shoulder. She thought of the surprise that both Ty and Matt had shown that she was still single. It was true, she was single by choice. It didn't feel like the easiest choice in the world right now, but she knew this was what she needed at this point. When she was ready, someone would come along. It was up to her to decide when to look.

Suddenly, Amy felt a pang of recognition – she didn't *want* to be back with Ty. It was hard to see him with someone new, but it wasn't fair to anyone for her to feel resentful about it. After all, she really had moved on, even if there wasn't a boy in her life to replace Ty. She knew she had to be OK with Ty moving on with life, too.

Amy looked away from Ty, and realized that there were a lot more people than usual at the open house. Gradually, she made her way around the room, chatting to old clients, local farmers, their feed suppliers. A friend of Nancy's introduced herself and offered to carry around some of the food. Matt waved at her across the room and toasted her formally with his glass of mulled cider.

Then, just when the house seemed to be bursting at the seams, Jack turned off the music and called for everyone's attention. The room went quiet, and Amy saw that Nancy was standing by his side, looking nervous. Amy felt her heart beating faster. What was going on?

"We're glad that so many of you have made it out this Christmas Eve," began Jack. "But I'm particularly glad that you've all been able to come, because Nancy and I have something very special to announce."

Amy looked around anxiously for Lou. Had she known about this? Surely it couldn't be bad news? Grandpa drew Nancy to his side and raised her left hand. Amy saw something sparkle on her ring finger. "I'm very, very happy to tell you all that we are now engaged."

There was a little gasp before applause and cheering broke out around the room. Amy felt her heart give a flip of relief and joy – and astonishment. Engaged! She rushed over to Jack and enveloped him in a hug, then turned and kissed Nancy, too.

"That is the best news ever," she declared. "I'm so happy for you, Grandpa. And you, Nancy. Congratulations!"

Nancy wiped away a tear. "Thank you, Amy," she said. "I'm glad you're happy. I was so worried about telling you."

"Worried! Why?" Amy shook her head in disbelief as Lou came over and hugged Grandpa, too.

"Jack and I haven't been able to agree about when to tell you," said Nancy. "I was so nervous about it. I wanted to tell you earlier, to get it out of the way, but Jack thought it would be better to make a big announcement."

"So *that's* what's been going on," said Amy, looking from one to the other of them. "And I thought something was really wrong!"

Jack put his arm around Nancy's shoulders, his face one big beaming smile. "Nothing wrong at all," he said. "I think I'm one of the happiest men on the planet."

Nancy smiled up at him. "You say the loveliest things, Jack," she said. Then she turned back to Amy and said more seriously, "I wanted to be sure we both felt this was the right thing to do, especially since it will have such an impact on your lives, too."

Amy clasped Nancy's hands, which felt smooth and warm. "You're part of our lives already, can't you see? We'd be lost without you."

"And hungry!" Scott chipped in, coming up with Holly propped on his shoulder.

As more people came up to offer their congratulations, Amy turned to Lou and gave her sister a hug. "I'm so glad," Lou said.

"I feel the same. And it's fabulous that there's someone who can make Grandpa so happy." Amy swallowed the lump that had grown in her throat. "A lot of things feel different this Christmas, Lou. But this is one change I'm totally happy about."

As Amy filled a guest's glass with the last of the mulled cider, she noticed that snow had begun to fall again outside, the flakes drifting slowly past the windowpanes. It was getting dark, and it would soon be time to get the evening chores done. She delivered the glass of cider, then pulled her boots on, grabbed a roll from the table, and headed outside.

Down in the barn, all was quiet. Some of the horses were dozing. Shalom had kicked her water bucket over, so Amy refilled it. Then she went up to the feed room to prepare the evening feeds. As she did, she heard the sound of one of the vehicles starting up and popped her head out to see who was leaving. It was Scott. Amy jogged over to see what the problem was.

"I got a call," he told her. "A horse, actually. Sounds like a simple case of colic, but you never know." He looked up at the sky. "I told Lou to stay here for the night with Holly. There's no telling how much more snow will fall before morning."

"OK, Scott," said Amy. "Drive safely. I'll be going over to the lumberyard later to check on Night Owl, and I'll call you if anything happens."

"Let's hope she waits for a couple more days," said Scott, putting his truck into gear. "Good luck. I'll be back tomorrow to wish you Merry Christmas!"

As he drove off the kitchen door opened and Ty walked out with Heather. "Amy!" he exclaimed. "You haven't been doing the chores on your own, have you?"

"It's no problem," said Amy. "I just started on the feeds, that's all."

"We'll give you a hand, then I'll drive you up to the

lumberyard to check on Night Owl," said Ty. He hesitated. "Heather would like to come, too. That's OK, isn't it?"

Amy's heart sank. "Sure," she said, trying not to sound guarded. She thought back on her realization in the living room and decided right then she'd make an effort to accept Heather more warmly from now on.

The snow seemed to be falling thicker all the time, and with no wind to sweep it into drifts, it was forming a thick blanket over everything. While Ty and Heather finished off the feeds, Amy checked over her foaling kit, then in a flash of inspiration, she went indoors to fill all the flasks they had with hot water. Most of the guests were beginning to leave to avoid getting snowed in. Amy told Grandpa, Lou, and Nancy where they were going, and Jack insisted that she take flashlights and a pile of blankets as well as her kit.

"You never know. You might need them," he said, and helped her carry them out to his pickup, where Ty and Heather were waiting in the cab.

The road up to the lumberyard was more treacherous than ever. A new layer of soft snow covering the icy first fall from the night before made it even harder for the tires on the pickup to get traction. Ty drove slowly, staying in low gear. Even with four-wheel drive, the pickup sometimes swerved from side to side before returning to the ruts it had followed before. Amy and Heather stayed quiet, staring ahead through the swishing windshield wipers.

As the hill got steeper, the pickup began to have more trouble, and at last Ty brought it to a halt. "We'll have to walk from here," he said.

Splitting the job of hauling the kit, blankets, and some more hay between them, they toiled up the last stretch of hill to the lumberyard. Amy was glad that Grandpa had insisted on the flashlights – they needed them to carve tunnels of light through the darkness and falling snow. But when a gust of wind stirred up the snow in their path, all Amy could see was light reflecting off the white.

They reached the yard out of breath but warmer because of the strenuous walk, and crunched their way over the snow to the little shed. Reuben heard them coming and began his squeaky bray of welcome. Amy pushed open the door and scanned the barn with her flashlight.

Night Owl was standing in one corner, but as Amy directed the light on to her body she shifted restlessly, twitching her tail.

"Hello, girl," said Amy. She placed her kit on the floor and approached her slowly to place her hand on her neck. Even in the cold night air, she could feel that the mare was sweating. She placed a hand on the horse's belly and felt something move beneath her fingers, then she checked beneath her tail, and looked at her udder. Drops of waxy colostrum glistened at the end of the teats. Now Amy was sure. She straightened up, and looked at Ty and Heather, who were watching her from the doorway.

"It's happening," she said, her heart pounding. "She's in labour."

Chapter Thirteen

It was seconds before anyone spoke.

"Wow," Heather whispered eventually.

"Are you sure?" asked Ty.

Night Owl began to pace around the barn, then stopped to urinate, her tail still twitching. "Yes." Amy trained her flashlight along the mare's body again. "Can you see how she's sunken behind the ribs, and her tail is jutting up more?"

"I'll go get some lanterns," said Heather. "There are a few left in the barn from the party."

"Thanks," said Amy. She let out a shaky breath. "I'd better call Scott."

With trembling fingers, she fished for her mobile and dialed Scott's number. To her dismay, the line was dead: A few short beeps told her that there was no reception. Amy stared down at her phone.

"Want me to try?" asked Ty.

"Yes, please!" Amy couldn't believe it. She'd known all along that Night Owl might go into labour in this makeshift stable, but she'd always assumed that she'd be be able to get ahold of Scott.

Ty punched in the number and put the phone to his ear. He soon frowned and took it away again. "Nothing," he said. "Maybe the weather's affected reception around here."

Amy swallowed. "Right," she said. "Well, we'll just have to hope that it's a straight-forward birth."

"You've studied foaling at college, though, haven't you?"

"Sure," she said, trying to sound more confident than she felt. "But I've never delivered a foal by myself before." *And certainly not two,* a little voice whispered in her mind – but she didn't give voice to it.

"I'm sure you'll manage." Ty smiled at her. "We'll do everything we can to help."

For a second, Amy felt a flash of warmth from the familiar knowledge that Ty was at her side, whatever she had to face. She took a deep breath. *Concentrate,* she told herself. *One step at a time. . .*

As Heather returned carrying two lanterns, Amy told her to place them out of the way of Night Owl's restless pacing, then opened up her kit bag and began to think. Fragments of her lectures returned as she looked around the barn.

"We should give her as much space as possible," she

told the others. "Ideally, mares like to give birth in private, with no one around. Sometimes they even delay the birth if they're feeling disturbed." She pointed at a shadowy part of the barn. "Let's sit over here. She'll be less aware of us then."

Ty and Heather moved the pile of blankets to the far corner of the barn.

"Should we just keep out of the way?" asked Ty as Amy gently examined Night Owl once again.

Amy nodded. "There's not a lot more we can do at this point. She's only in the first stage of labor, which could go on for hours. We just have to keep a close eye on what's happening in case anything goes wrong."

With the snow still falling outside, it would have been very cold to hang around waiting if it weren't for the blankets. Heather went on another trip to the barn and came back with a tarp, which they placed on top to act as an extra layer of insulation. Then she settled down with Ty on a pile of straw and pulled the warm covers over them. Amy hesitated, then joined them. It was all a bit too intimate for her liking, but the biting cold gave her little choice.

Now, they just had to watch. Amy had positioned one of the lanterns so that it cast a soft glow over the area where

Night Owl was pacing around, without being too intrusive or glaring, and placed the other near where they were sitting. Reuben, puzzled at first by all the activity, came and nosed them curiously, but soon decided that they were not as interesting as the new batch of hay.

An hour passed. Heather had a little radio with her and they turned it on to a station that was playing carols, watching to see whether it disturbed the mare. It didn't seem to. If anything, it seemed to soothe her slightly and she pricked her ears. But then her contractions began again, and she returned to pacing to and fro, ignoring the little huddle of people in the corner.

Nine o'clock . . . ten o'clock . . . ten-thirty . . . The time ticked by slower and slower. Heather yawned and became drowsy, leaning her head on Ty's shoulder, and Amy began to feel sleepy, too. But then, sometime after eleven o'clock, Night Owl stopped pacing and lay down on the straw with a grunt.

"I think this is it," Amy whispered.

Fully alert now, she watched as the mare stretched out her legs, contractions rippling her belly. A gush of fluid trickled on to the straw, and Amy knew that her water had broken.

"How long should it take from now?" asked Heather,

her eyes wide with awe.

"Not long," replied Amy. "Fifteen minutes, maybe. It could be much quicker. I won't intervene unless it looks as though she's in trouble."

Quietly, she stood up and crept towards the mare to get a closer look. She knew what should happen if the birth was normal: The two front feet would appear first, the hooves facing downward, one slightly in front of the other. The nose would be tucked down on to the front legs, close to the knees.

A big contraction wracked Night Owl's body. Amy peered underneath her tail and saw a tiny hoof appear. Ty and Heather crept alongside her, and Heather gasped when she saw the hoof.

"This is so awesome," she whispered.

Amy nodded, unable to speak. It was incredibly special to see a birth happening like this. But as more of the hoof showed, followed by the foreleg, she frowned. Where was the other hoof? They should both have appeared together. Night Owl stirred on the straw, the whites of her eyes showing as she looked around at her belly. Amy waited until another contraction had passed, but there was still no sign of the second hoof.

"Something's wrong," she said. "The other foreleg's

stuck. I'm going to have to try and help her." She glanced around at Ty and Heather. Their faces were solemn, and Heather looked pale.

"Just tell us what to do," said Ty.

"OK." Amy took a deep breath. "Let's get my kit. I'll need the rubber gloves and a bucket with some warm water and disinfectant."

Without another word, Ty and Heather set to work. Ty located the rubber gloves in the kit bag, while Heather began opening the flasks and pouring hot water into the bucket. Meanwhile Amy checked the mare's pulse. It was getting faster – a sure sign that she was in distress. She bit her lip. She'd never had to do anything like this during her college training. Hurriedly, she fumbled for her mobile again, hoping that Scott had come within range.

The line was still dead. Ty met her gaze and smiled.

"You can do it, Amy," he said, handing her the gloves. "We believe in you."

Heather nodded. "We really do."

Amy looked up at their faces, both full of encouragement. Her gaze rested on Ty's for a second longer, thinking of all the times he had been there for her. Times of crisis and heartache. Times of disaster. Times when a horse was in danger. Times like this. And she knew that even with

Heather standing next to him, there was no one in the whole world that she trusted more.

She knelt down beside the mare, pulling on the rubber gloves. She knew what she had to do: She had to locate the second foreleg, untrap it if it was trapped and pull it forward to lie alongside the other one. Her fingers trembling, she reached inside the mare, feeling along the line of the first leg, searching for the other. There was nothing. It must be bent right back. No one spoke. Night Owl gave a restless kick with her hind legs, then slumped her head down, breathing heavily.

Heather went and sat by the mare's head, murmuring reassurances and stroking her cheek. Amy pushed her fingers a little farther, and to her relief, she felt the second leg. The tiny knobby knee was bent back, and she wrapped her fingers around it.

"Have you got it?" asked Ty.

Amy realized she'd been holding her breath. She let it out and gently eased the foreleg forward. "Here it comes," she muttered.

With the foreleg finally in the right position, Amy withdrew her hand. Night Owl pushed again, and to Amy's delight, both little hooves jutted out into the cold air.

"Hey," murmured Ty, his voice full of admiration. "You

did it."

Amy glanced up at him, and their eyes locked. For a moment all the tension of the last few days evaporated. They were a team again. She smiled. "It's not over yet," she said. She looked up at Heather, who was still holding the mare's head. "Let's give her some space."

Quietly, the three of them retreated a few feet and watched. With the next push, a little nose appeared, resting on the foal's knees, followed by the whole of its head. Night Owl rested for a moment, then, with another heave, half the body slithered out.

"Should we help her?" asked Heather. "She must be so tired."

Amy shook her head. "No. Let her do it naturally. It's safer that way."

With a final push, the rest of the foal slid out on to the straw, the umbilical cord behind trailing it. The foal had already broken through the sac that enclosed it, so Amy simply wiped its nose and mouth clear, checked that it had started to breathe, then let it lie still for a while. It was bay, with a white stripe. Reuben, curious about what was happening, tried to nose his way forward, and Ty gently restrained him.

"See how the umbilical cord is still pulsing?" Amy

pointed out. "We can't cut it until that stops. The foal's still getting blood from the mare."

"Wow," Heather said again.

They waited for a few moments, watching the foal take its first breaths.

Suddenly, Ty pointed at the mare. "Amy – what's happening?" he asked, sounding alarmed. "That's not the afterbirth, is it?"

A strong contraction ran along Night Owl's flank – much stronger than she'd need to eject the placenta. Amy's heart lurched. She'd been right. Another set of hooves had appeared beneath the mare's tail.

"Oh, my goodness!" Heather gasped. "I didn't think horses had twins!"

Amy felt her body break into a sweat, wishing that she'd thought through her hunch more carefully. "It's really rare," she said. "It's particularly rare for a mare to go full-term." She swallowed. "That must be why she's giving birth early, before her owners expect her to. I guess they'll be as surprised as we are."

If these foals were premature, they would probably be weak. The first foal seemed healthy enough, though he was perhaps a little on the small side. She'd have to check him over once the umbilical cord had been cut.

But this second one . . . She watched as the little head emerged from Night Owl's rear, followed by the rest of its body. The birth was quicker than the first one had been, and with her heart beating faster, Amy could see why.

"It's tiny!" Ty exclaimed, voicing her thoughts.

The dark grey foal was only about two-thirds of the size of the first one. And whereas the first was now beginning to stir and twitch its hooves, this one looked sickly and listless.

"Is it dead?" Heather whispered.

Amy couldn't let herself think that. She simply had to act. Her reflexes took over and she set to work briskly, clearing the tiny foal's nose and mouth.

"Could you pass me the towel, please?" she asked Ty, indicating her kit.

Ty passed it to her, and she used it to rub the foal vigorously, drying off the mucus that covered it and trying to stimulate it to start breathing properly. Only then did she look up at Ty and Heather again, and saw the strain on their faces as they waited for her to speak.

"No, it's not dead," she said, glancing quickly at each of them in turn. "It's breathing."

Ty's face split into a smile, and Heather heaved a sigh of

relief.

The first foal was now on its feet. Once she was sure that the second foal was breathing of its own accord, Amy reached for her scissors. She checked to be sure the flow from the mare had stopped and then cut the umbilical cord of the first one and disinfected the end with iodine. She did the same for the second foal, as Night Owl began to struggle to her feet.

"Let's stand back now," said Amy. "She'll want to lick them."

They watched as Night Owl turned towards her babies, her ears pricked in curiosity. Amy felt a lump rise in her throat as the mare whickered and began to lick them, nosing them gently with her muzzle.

"We should give them names," she murmured.

At that moment, a peal of bells sounded on the radio, filling the little barn. It was midnight. It was Christmas Day.

"We could name the bay one Carillon," suggested Heather. "It means a peal of bells."

Amy smiled. "That's perfect," she said. She looked down at the smaller foal, still lying on the straw. "And how about Moonlight for this little fella?"

"That's lovely," Heather declared. "Merry Christmas,

everyone!"

She turned to hug Ty, and Amy watched. Heather had been so helpful and friendly tonight. And Ty . . . Ty had been the way he always was: kind, dependable, totally on her side. Amy knew that she didn't begrudge Ty's new relationship. Friendship was a gift in itself, and she could still have the friendship she wanted with Ty. Their connection would last forever, but it would take a different shape from now on.

Heather and Ty pulled apart, and Ty turned to hug Amy. She let him take her in his arms and hold her close.

"Merry Christmas, Amy," he murmured.

Amy looked up at him. "And to you, too," she replied. She pulled free and held one arm out to Heather, who was standing awkwardly off to the side. "Merry Christmas, Heather. Welcome to the team."

Heather's face broke into a smile. The two girls hugged, and Amy met Ty's gaze over Heather's shoulder. He smiled and Amy knew that their work at Heartland was bigger than all their personal feelings. They would always, always share that priority, which set them apart from anyone else.

Carillon was struggling to his feet, his legs wobbling desperately as he made his way to the mare's udder. But

Moonlight showed no signs of getting up, and sadness welled up inside Amy. There was something she hadn't told Heather and Ty. She'd chosen the name Moonlight for a reason. As she'd tried to rub life into his tiny grey body, she discovered just how frail he was. The muscles and bones were underdeveloped, and the heartbeat was like the flutter of a bird. She'd realized then that this little creature would never see the light of day.

Over the next half hour, the mare pushed the afterbirth out of her body, and Amy checked it carefully to make sure it was all there. She also made sure that Carillon had started to nurse properly to receive the colostrum – the first milk that contained vital antibodies that would help the foal fight disease. Moonlight still lay stretched out on the straw.

"Why isn't Moonlight getting up the way Carillon did?" asked Heather. "Is he going to be OK?"

Amy bent over the tiny foal and felt for his heartbeat again. Maybe there was still hope – maybe he could pull through. But the shallow, irregular pulsing told her all she needed to know. It was even weaker now. With a heavy heart, she straightened up and prepared to give Ty and Heather the news. From the expression on Ty's face, she could tell he had already guessed what she would say.

"Moonlight's not going to survive," she said quietly. "There's nothing we can do. He's just too weak. Carillon had the lion's share of the nutrients in the womb – that's what happens a lot of the time with twins. Moonlight's limbs and organs simply haven't developed enough."

Silence fell. Then Heather's lip wobbled. "Poor little thing," she said. "There's really nothing we can do?"

Amy shook her head. She knew that this would be the hardest part of being a vet – acknowledging that some animals were beyond her reach. "He won't have the strength to stand and nurse," she said. "We just have to make sure that Carillon gets everything he needs, and meanwhile make Moonlight as comfortable as possible."

"How can we do that? Is he in pain?" Heather's eyes were wide with anguish.

"No, he's not suffering." That was some comfort, at least. "A blanket to keep him warm will make him sleepy. He'll just drift away."

Heather picked up one of the blankets and laid it over the little foal, then sat down on the straw next to him. Ty sat beside her, putting his arm around her. Amy turned her attention to Night Owl, encouraging the mare to pay attention to Carillon. Although he was slightly undersize,

Carillon sucked eagerly at Night Owl's teats with his stubby tail waggling. She watched the bond between them growing before her eyes, and smiled. They would be just fine.

By the time she was ready to settle down next to Heather and Ty on the straw, Amy realized that it was two in the morning. Reuben the donkey had started to doze, a tuft of hay dangled from his rubbery lips. Heather was stroking Moonlight's ears.

"How's he doing?" Amy asked.

Heather looked up at her. "I think he just stopped breathing," she replied, a tremble in her voice.

Amy knelt down and checked the foal for a pulse. "Yes," she said. "He's gone."

Heather's eyes filled with tears. "I can't believe how . . . how *peaceful* it was," she said.

Amy smiled at her. "You helped," she said. "I'm sure it was a comfort to him to have someone there. He would have known he wasn't alone."

Heather bit her lip, then lifted the edge of the blanket and pulled it over the foal's head so that he was completely covered.

Ty got up and peered out of the barn. "It stopped snowing," he said.

"Do you think we should try to get back to Heartland?" asked Heather.

Amy shook her head. "No. I want to keep an eye on Night Owl and Carillon. We could try to get some sleep, though."

Ty turned to look at her, his green eyes full of warmth. "You did an amazing job tonight, Amy," he said. "You are going to be a fantastic vet."

"I feel so lucky to have been here," added Heather.

Amy felt her cheeks flush. "Well, I couldn't have done it without you guys," she said. She hesitated, then added, "Like I said. We're a team."

The sound of a vehicle broke into Amy's dreams. She opened her eyes. Daylight was filtering into the barn, and her neck was stiff from lying awkwardly on the straw. She sat up, rubbing it.

Ty was standing by the barn door, and Heather was still asleep, her blond hair just peeking out from underneath one of the blankets.

"Did I hear something?" said Amy.

"I think it might be Scott," said Ty. He opened the door. "I'll go check."

"How long have I been asleep? Is everything OK?"

asked Amy. She looked over at Night Owl, who was pulling at the hay net alongside Reuben. Carillon was curled up on the straw, asleep.

"Everything's fine." Ty smiled at her.

Amy returned his smile and scrambled to her feet. "Wait – I'll come with you."

Scott reached them first. There was the sound of boots crunching through the snow, and then his familiar face looked through the door. Heather stirred and sat up, bits of straw sticking out of her hair.

"Hey! I found you," Scott exclaimed, letting himself into the barn. "And all safe and sound, by the looks of things."

"Scott! It's so good to see you!" Amy exclaimed. "We tried to get hold of you last night – Night Owl gave birth to twins. . ."

"Twins!" Scott's eyebrows shot up. He took in the scene, including the little form still covered in a blanket. His face sobered. "And one of them didn't make it?"

"Neither of them would have, if it hadn't been for Amy," Ty said. "One of the front legs on the healthy foal was bent back. She turned it around."

Scott looked impressed. "Can't have been easy," he commented. "You did well to save just one of them."

He approached Night Owl and examined her, then turned to Carillon. "You checked the placenta, I take it?" he said, running his hand over the foal's body.

Amy nodded. "Yes, it's all there."

Scott straightened up, looking at the three tired faces. "You all did amazingly," he said. "Now, I think you should get back to Heartland. I'll take care of things here."

"Thanks, Scott," said Amy. "Are you sure there's nothing more we can do?"

Scott shook his head. "Everything is just as it should be," he said. "It's sad about the second foal, but the first one's doing well – and that's a miracle in itself."

Later that morning, as Jack served up a full breakfast, Grandpa and Nancy's announcement seemed like a dream – so much had happened since then. But it was real, all right. Nancy's face was radiant as she buzzed around the kitchen, the diamond on her finger twinkling at every turn.

Amy, Ty, and Heather dug into piles of crispy bacon, golden-yolked eggs, and sausages.

"Not the most traditional Christmas Day meal," smiled Jack, adding a little mound of sautéed mushrooms to everyone's plate. "We'll just have to eat the turkey this evening. Couldn't keep you waiting – you all looked famished when you came in!"

"It's perfect, Grandpa," Amy declared.

Lou came through from the office with Holly on her hip, and swung her into the high chair. "Mrs. Cheshire called while you were on your way back," she told them. "I gave her the news, and she got in touch with Night Owl's owners. They're cutting their trip short to come back and care for their new foal."

"That's great news!" said Amy. "It must be a big surprise for them."

"Yes," agreed Lou, putting a little spoon into Holly's hand. "They're so relieved that mare and foal survived. They said it's the best Christmas gift ever. Apparently, they had no idea about the twins."

Nancy poured glasses of orange juice and handed them around. "Well, I think they have a lot to be grateful for. You three did an amazing job to save them." She smiled in turn at Amy, Ty, and Heather.

Holly squealed and banged her spoon on her high chair, making everyone laugh. Amy reached for her glass, catching Ty's eye as she did. Something else had happened last night, and she sensed that Ty could feel it, too. Quite simply, they'd moved on. She and Ty would always be friends – and they'd always be able to work together closely, understanding what a horse or a pony needed, understanding what Heartland needed. But there was someone new to help them now, and that was Heather.

She raised her glass. "Merry Christmas, everyone!"

"Merry Christmas!"